Manual of the Core Value Workshop

ISBN 0-9744390-1-0
CompassionPower
20139 Laurel Hill Way
Germantown, MD 20874
301-921-2010
CompassionPower.com

Booksurge, LLC
5341Dorchester Rd., Suite16
North Charleston, SC29418

Manual of the Core Value Workshop

Steven Stosny, Ph.D.

Also by Steven Stosny

You Don't Have to Take It Anymore:
Turn Your Resentful, Angry, or Emotionally Abusive Relationship into a Compassionate, Loving One

How to Improve Your Marriage without talking about It: Finding Love beyond Words

Treating Attachment Abuse: A Compassionate Approach

The Powerful Self

My Good Heart
Drawing book for ages 5-9

Power Quest CD-ROM for adolescents

Compassionate Eating CD-ROM

HEALS CD-ROM

Contents

To My Mother, Barbara McCrocklin
Her pain inspired this work,
Her ideas helped shape it
Her compassion gave it life

Session 1: *Ending the Pain*

Blame makes you powerless.
Responsibility gives you the power to make your life better.

Please do not lose this opportunity to make significant gains in your life. (There is no tragedy like lost opportunity for growth and healing.) To grow and heal, you must remove the magnifying glass from others, and focus it exclusively on you.

- Learn at least one thing from every paragraph of the manual.
- Reward yourself for every single thing you learn.
- Recognize the enormous power of the knowledge you gain.

Note: The content of this course will be harder to learn and practice during alcohol and drug use. Alcohol and drugs numb the regulatory part of the brain, making impulses stronger and regulation weaker. If you feel you may have an alcohol or drug problem, tell your instructor in private.

This is a greatly accelerated course. Thirty-six weeks of material is crammed into 14 weeks. You won't share your experience or problems in this group. (You do that in the homework.) In class you will learn information and acquire tools to solve your problems in *self-empowering* and *compassionate* ways. You will learn self-regulation to act in your best interest, *regardless* of what anyone else does.

By the time you've completed all the work of this course, you will feel more powerful than you have ever felt. You will experience *genuine power.*

Genuine Power

Power is not just the ability to do something or to get someone else to do something. For instance, you have the power to drive your car into the side of a building, and you might even be able to coerce your significant other into doing the same. But would you be powerful if you did that?

Shooting yourself in the foot is not power.

Power is the ability to act in your long-term best interest. It is behaving according to what you believe to be the most important things about you as a person. If you were to write down the most important thing about you as a person, you would not write, "hurting the people I love."

Whenever We Hurt a Loved One, We Bleed a Little Inside.

Imagine the most hurtful thing you ever said or did to someone you love.

Now imagine a stranger saying or doing that same thing to that person. What would your response be?

We have an unconscious and automatic instinct to protect those we love. When we see them harmed, we feel anger, aggressive impulses, and at least temporary loathing for the person hurting them. What happens to that anger, aggression, and hatred when *you* are the one harming those you must protect? Where do the anger, aggression, and loathing go?

The legacy of family abuse is self-loathing.

The human species could not have survived without the instinct to protect loved ones. That instinct is so strong that **you *cannot* feel good about yourself when you hurt someone you love.**

No One Escapes the Effects of Abuse

- Everyone in an abusive family loses some degree of dignity and autonomy (the ability to decide one's own thoughts, feelings, and behavior).

- At least half of victims, abusers, and children in abusive families suffer from clinical anxiety and/or depression. ("Clinical" means that it interferes with normal functioning.)

- Most victims, abusers, and children lack genuine self-esteem.

- Emotional abuse is usually more psychologically damaging than physical abuse.

- Abuse tends to get worse without intervention from someone outside the family.

- Witnessing abuse makes a child 10 times more likely to become either an abuser or a victim of abuse. As adults they are at increased risk of alcoholism, criminality, mental health problems, and poverty.

- Symptoms of children in abusive families include one or more of the following: depression (looks like chronic boredom), anxiety, school problems, aggressiveness, hyperactivity, low self-esteem, over emotionality (anger, excitability, or frequent crying), or no emotions at all. (If your children have any of these symptoms, the best thing you can do for them is practice what you learn in this course. When *you* get better, they will almost always get better. Children learn to regulate their emotions by watching their parents. It's called *modeling*.)

- Witnessing a parent victimized is usually more psychologically damaging to children than injuries from direct child abuse. Seeing a parent abused *is* child abuse.

- Symptoms of victims and abusers often include one or more of the following:
  - Trouble sleeping
  - Frequent periods of sadness and crying
  - Continual worry, anxiety, or excessive anger
  - Obsessions (thoughts you can't get out of your mind)
  - Confusion/impaired decision-making.

Important questions to ask of yourself (The goal of the course is for you to answer a resounding yes):

- Do I like myself?
- Am I able to realize my potential?
- Does everyone I care about feel safe?
- Do my children like themselves?
- Are they able to realize their fullest potential?
- Do they feel safe?

Bill of Rights

No one, under any circumstance, deserves to feel disregarded, insulted, controlled, coerced, intimidated, hurt, hit, pushed, grabbed, or touched in *any* undesired way.

Nothing that anyone says or does can justify abuse.
One act of abuse never justifies another.

Why is it not okay to hit back or call a name back?

Failures of Compassion

All abuse begins with a *failure* of *self-compassion.* You fail to understand and heal your hurt, which then turns into resentment, anger and an impulse to control others. As you blame your core hurts on someone else, you begin hurting the feelings of loved ones, at first by failing to understand them. That starts you on a downward spiral of abuse.

The Downward Spiral of Abuse

Hurting the feelings of loved ones (accidentally or on purpose)

Criticizing personality (instead of behavior)

Attacking self-esteem

Insulting or Name-Calling

Controlling/Manipulating

Isolating, discouraging friends

Coercing, threatening, intimidating

Destroying property

Threatening or harming pets

Grabbing, pushing, shoving, slapping

Kicking, burning, biting, punching

Hitting with object

Using or threatening use of weapons

Death

By enhancing self-compassion, which you will do in the first part of this course, compassion for loved ones follows *automatically*. When you control minor abuse, the more severe forms on the downward spiral of abuse never happen.

Emergency Tactics

Before you learn more advanced skill, use the following emergency tactics to avoid hurting yourself and those you love. Go over them with your loved ones if possible.

- Know that you have the absolute power to keep from hurting people you love, even though you feel hurt and angry. There is no such thing as uncontrollable anger. (The only uncontrollable condition is psychosis, which requires indefinite, court-ordered hospitalization.) You have a lot more *inner-strength* than the lashing-out response of anger.

- There is no such thing as a safe level of family violence. The home is the most dangerous place to have physical altercations, in terms of things to fall over, places to crack heads and bones, and lethal objects to throw. Serious injury and death occur frequently from little force, with no intent to do serious harm.

- Know your early aggression signs (what it feels like in your head, eyes, mouth, neck, shoulders, chest, back, and hands). Your body gets ready for aggression about 5,000 times faster than your conscious mind knows that you feel aggressive.

- When you feel aggressive, ask yourself, "*How can you make this better?*" Once you ask yourself this question, you *cannot* be abusive.

- Take a time-out (leave the room or the house). **Set up the time-out strategy with your family members when you go home tonight**, so that everyone knows what you are doing. Say *respectfully*:

  "I need a time-out to regulate my anger."

  "I would like to continue to talk about this once I feel calm, at about _____ (give a specific time)."

  It's important that you do not wait until you need it to spring the time-out rules on your loved ones. **Be sure to set it up in advance.** You will soon learn more powerful techniques, but it takes a while to master them. For now, use time-outs.

- If anyone in the family is afraid of violence, call the police.

- If violence is not a threat, but you are hurting each other emotionally, call your local hotline number.

The Power of Attachment

In attachment relationships we form emotional bonds with significant others, including children, parents, lovers, and sometimes brothers, sisters, and good friends. These deep emotional bonds give enormous power to participants of attachment relationships. They *build* the sense of self. We learn how important, valuable, loving, and worthy of love we are only by interacting with those we love.

The crucial elements of ***self-building*** in attachment relationships are:

1. Unconditional safety and security for all parties;
2. High levels of compassion;
3. Freedom from resentment, hostility, abuse, and other emotional constraints.

If a relationship consistently fails in any of the above, it loses its self-building function and does more harm than good.

If it falls below the threshold of safety and security, it becomes ***self-destroying***.

Once that happens, only self-compassion and emotional conditioning can rebuild the sense of self. Only consistent compassion on the part of the abuser can rebuild abusive relationships.

Compassion

The word, "compassion," as used in this book, does not refer to Mother Theresa kind of compassion. Research shows that for healthy relationships, compassion for others must be **in balance** with **self-compassion.** Other people are equally valuable but no more valuable than you.

Self-compassion requires **assertiveness** – standing up for your rights and feelings. The difference between assertiveness and aggression is that assertiveness respects the rights and feelings of others, while aggression disrespects and devalues the rights of others.

Compassion is:

- More important than love (Love without compassion is controlling, possessive, even dangerous.)

- Sympathetic understanding of your own core hurts and those of others

- Caring about others, because it makes *you* feel worthy of love

- Recognizing the Core Value of self and others, even when you don't like their behavior or disagree with their perspectives

- Motivation to do the right thing

- Not the same as forgiveness or condoning offenses

- Not the same as reinstating relationships. (It can be just in your head.)

Emotional Inhibitors

Next week you will learn how anger mobilizes the entire central nervous system, every muscle group, and each organ of the body for one purpose: fighting. Consequently, anger-driven behavior is the most socially controlled, legally punished, and religiously prohibited of human experience.

What do you think is the most common *emotional inhibitor* of anger? What usually keeps us from busting someone in the mouth when angry?

It's usually *fear of consequences*. We might get angry enough at our spouses to hit them if they say certain things about us. Yet we would find a way not to be so angry if Mike Tyson said the exact same things.

The problem with fear of consequences as an emotional inhibitor is that it erodes self-esteem. If fear of going to jail is the only reason you do not hurt your family, you will not feel good about yourself. The only reliable emotional regulator is one that keeps you true to your deepest values, which includes **compassion** for those you love.

But there is a problem with the healing power of compassion. It gets turned off by hurt. The more hurt you feel, the harder it is to feel compassion.

Self-Compassion

Self-compassion is the necessary step to compassion for others and emotional well being.

Self-compassion is:

- Understanding that when you are angry, resentful, anxious, or depressed, you are feeling hurt or afraid that you might be hurt
- Sympathy with your hurt
- Motivation to make yourself feel more valuable and worthy

Spend the next week understanding your deeper emotions (beneath anger, resentment, and worry), and how you can make your situation or your experience of your situation better.

SESSION 2: *Core Value*

Core Value is the drive to create value. Present in all humans at birth, it is the instinctual self-worth that makes newborns value and attach to caregivers, with the expectation that their emotional needs will be met by their caregivers.

Throughout life, Core Value tells us how important, valuable, loving, and lovable we are, as it forms the foundation of personal security, well being, self-esteem, competence, creativity, and power.

Core Value is the deepest experience of the self. It is awareness of your **humanity. When in touch with Core Value, you cannot do wrong.**

Core Value is an emotional awareness that no problem, behavior, or event can reduce your value as a person. It is a deep feeling that you are valuable enough to change any behavior that is harmful to you or to someone you love.

Core Value is *invincible* to damage from the outside world. The world can cause you expense and inconvenience, it can hurt your feelings and body, but it can *never* hurt your Core Value.

While you can never lose Core Value, you can lose touch with it. **The impulse to control or harm tells you that your current state of Core Value is too low.** The impulse to control or harm does *not* tell you that you need more power; it tells you that you need more Core Value. It's like a gas gauge showing that your Core Value is on empty and that you need to fill it up!

Statement of Core Value

(Read aloud)

I am worthy of respect, value, and compassion, whether or not I get them from others. If I don't get them from others, it is necessary to feel <u>more</u> worthy, not <u>less</u>. It is necessary to affirm my own deep value as a unique person (a child of God). I respect and value myself. I have compassion for my hurt. I have compassion for the hurt of others. I trust myself to act in my best interests and in the best interests of loved ones.

Improve, Appreciate, Connect, Protect

Although sometimes experienced as a sense of humanity, intimacy, community, or spirituality, people experience Core Value most frequently as motivation to **improve, appreciate, protect,** or **connect**.

How you feel from moment to moment is determined by the current state of your Core Value. To feel good, you must improve, appreciate, protect, or connect. If you do one, you feel better. If you do two, you feel much better, and if you do all, you feel joy. If you do none, you feel numb. If you violate one, you feel bad. If you violate two, you feel worse, and if you violate all, you feel resentful, depressed, angry, or anxious.

Core Value Exercise

Here's an exercise to invoke Core Value and keep it in reserve for whenever you need it.

Imagine that you're driving by yourself, and just ahead you see a car lose control and crash into a tree. Two people are in the car, a mother and a four year-old child. The mother is unhurt, but she's trapped in the front seat and cannot help her child, who climbs out the back window. Though unhurt, she feels helpless and panicky. You are the only car close to the victims. What will you do?

Of course, most people would call 911, reassure the mother that help is on the way, and comfort the child.

Imagine that you've done the first two, and now you're comforting the child. You tell her it will be okay, her mother is fine. You very much want to make her feel better. It's become so important to you to comfort her that you don't notice right away how it's working.

- The child is calming down and starting to feel okay
- She holds tightly onto you, arms around you neck, her head on your chest
- She now feels peaceful and good, because of you.

As you imagine helping the mother and comforting the child, you experience your Core Value. This image will overcome any impatience, resentment, or anger you experience. It will help you to act always in your best interest.

Core Value is a light within you. You will learn to activate it *anytime* you feel impatient, resentful, or angry.

From Your Core Value

You Protect the Safety of Everyone You Love

Power Statement

Read the following aloud, and feel the *power* in your words as you reclaim control of your emotions and your deepest values:

I WILL WORK HARD TO HEAL MY HURT. THIS MEANS UNDERSTANDING MY OWN DEEPEST EMOTIONS AND THOSE OF ALL MY LOVED ONES. I WILL NOT HURT THEIR FEELINGS OR TRY TO CONTROL THEM, EVEN IF THEY HURT MINE OR TRY TO CONTROL ME.

Core Value Bank

The *Core Value Bank* is designed as a repository of your core value, a kind of bank account of important things. You can think of each of the eight segments as a safety deposit box containing images or icons of some of the most important things to and about you. The Core Value Bank is itself an image of your *internal* value. The images it contains, while they might correspond to things in the world, reside *within* you. They are *always* there, ready to give you strength whenever you need it. Each time you see, hear, smell, touch, or taste something in the world similar to the contents of your Core Value Bank, it will remind you of your core value and thereby activate it. In other words, you will be motivated to improve, appreciate, connect, or protect. The next time you see a sunset, for example, it will not only seem beautiful, it will remind you of your core value.

The best thing about the Core Value Bank is that you make deposits at the same time you make withdrawals. You will *never* run out of core value.

After you fill in the boxes, we'll put your Bank to use as a tool of emotional reconditioning. Get ready for magic.

Your **basic humanity** safe deposit box is already filled in. This is the emotion you felt when you imagined helping and comforting the desperate child.

Meaning and purpose statements:

1. The *most* important thing about you as a person.
2. The *most* important thing about your life in general.

Love: Fill in the names of your loved ones. You're writing their names, but the emotional content of this box will be the actual love you feel for them.

Spiritual: Fill in a symbol (a drawing, mark, or word will do) of something that has spiritual importance to you. It can be religious, natural, cosmic, or social – anything will do, as long as it connects you to something larger than the self, which, while you are connected to it, seems more important than your everyday, mundane, or selfish concerns.

Nature: Name, draw, or describe a nature scene that makes you value, i.e., something that you feel is beautiful.

Creativity: Identify a piece of art, music, or other human creation that makes you feel value.

Community: Identify a sense of community connection, for example, a church, school, work, or neighborhood.

Compassion: List three compassionate things you have done. Don't think of Mother Theresa kind of compassion. These can be relatively small gestures, when you helped or comforted someone else, with no material gain to you.

My Core Value Bank

Basic Humanity	Meaning & Purpose	Love	Spiritual
The emotions I felt as I imagined rescuing and comforting the desperate child:	The most important thing about me as a person: The most important thing about my life in general:	The people I love:	My spiritual connection:
Nature	**Creativity**	**Community**	**Compassion**
Something beautiful in nature:	Something beautiful human made (art, music, architecture, furniture, etc.):	My community connection:	Compassionate things I have done: 1. 2. 3.

Emotional Conditioning

A simple way to practice emotional conditioning is to connect your Core Value to any devaluing experience, either at the moment it happens or after the fact. When irritating things happen, experience the light of your Core Value and invoke the emotions of your Core Value Bank. **Practice with *each* of the following situations.**

1. You're running late, the car ahead of you won't get out of your way. **Experience your Core Value – the emotional content of your Core Value Bank. Feel the light of Core Value.**

2. Someone cuts you off. **Experience your Core Value – the emotional content of your Core Value Bank. Feel the light of Core Value.**

3. The traffic totally jams up. **Experience your Core Value – the emotional content of your Core Value Bank. Feel the light of Core Value.**

4. A guy in another car gestures and yells at you. **Experience your Core Value – the emotional content of your Core Value Bank. Feel the light of Core Value.**

5. Somebody is tailgating you. **Experience your Core Value – the emotional content of your Core Value Bank. Feel the light of Core Value.**

6. A jerk leans on the horn. **Experience your Core Value – the emotional content of your Core Value Bank. Feel the light of Core Value.**

7. A van speeds by too close to you. **Experience your Core Value – the emotional content of your Core Value Bank. Feel the light of Core Value.**

Reconnect to Core Value at Least 12 Times per Day

The ultimate goal is to stay connected to Core Value all the time. In the beginning, you will need to remember to invoke Core Value. Have certain places that automatically remind you. The bedroom and car are good places to start. Whenever you go into your bedroom, whenever you get into your car, connect to your Core Value.

It is important to connect to Core Value when you do not really need to, so that it will become easier to connect to it under stress.

Wear your **Core Value** like a medal of honor.

Aggressive Behavior

Core hurts are not usually active. But when they are, they cause an abrupt drop in self-value. Many people learned early in life to protect against the drop in self-value with some form of anger, resentment, or aggression. The motivation to avoid or numb core hurts causes all harmful behavior.

Core Hurts

Disregarded
Unimportant
Accused
Guilty
Devalued
Rejected
Powerless
Inadequate/Unlovable

The Three Levels of the Emotional Self

There are three levels of the emotional self. The top layer is what the world sees. On the good side this layer includes interest, enjoyment, compassion, love, etc. On the bad side it includes blame, anger, anxiety, obsessions, depression, manipulations, control, alcohol and drug use, etc. Always deeper than these negative states are core hurts. If core hurts do not activate Core Value, they activate the top layer of negative states.

Of course no one was born with core hurts, although we've all learned them. Always deeper than core hurts is your birthright of Core Value. If you go deeply enough into yourself, you must come to Core Value.

Blame, Anger, Obsessions, Manipulation, Control, Alcohol, Abuse of Self & Others

CORE HURTS

Core Value

Self-compassion activates your Core Value and ensures your best interest.

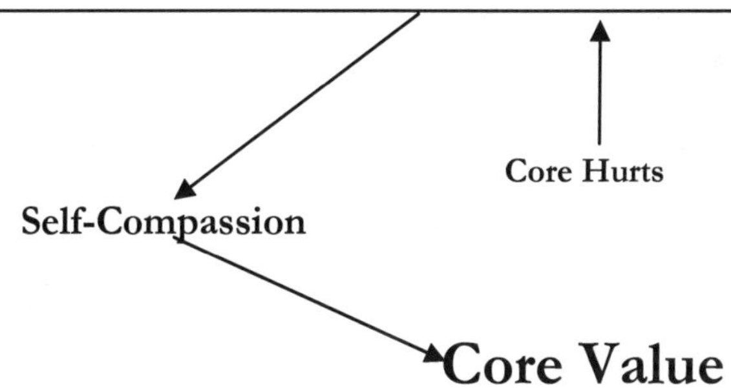

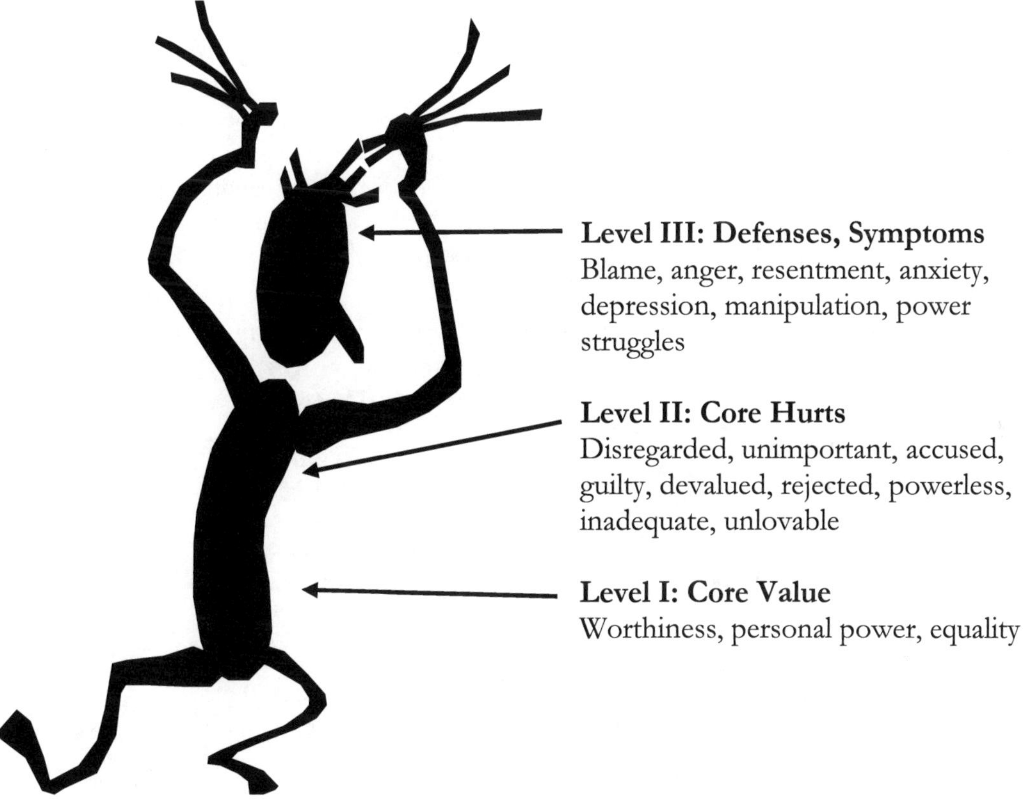

Core Hurts and Abuse in Relationships

The impulse to control and abuse begins with core hurts and failure of self-compassion. We tend to hurt people we love when we feel unlovable. **In the history of human kind has anyone ever felt more lovable by hurting someone he loves?**

If a loved one triggers a core hurt in you, it is most likely because she feels unlovable. **In the history of human kind has anyone ever felt more lovable being hurt by someone she loves?**

In this course you will learn to respond to core hurts with Core Value and see that the real problem in your angry or resentful disagreements with a loved one is that you both feel unlovable. When you understand that, aggressive and controlling behaviors cannot be options.

Anger Problems

Anger is the most self-revealing emotion. It points directly to your current state of Core Value.

One dangerous myth about an "anger problem" is that it only involves aggression, abuse, hurting people, or destroying property. This describes only *one* of *many* forms of anger problems.

You can develop an anger problem from the recurrence of a subtle form of anger that you may not even notice. Problem anger *makes* you do something that is not in your best interest or *keeps* you from doing what is in your best interest. This could be simply putting a chilly wall between you and your loved ones, or a continual impatience that keeps you from feeling compassion for loved ones and from gaining their compassion.

One sure sign of an anger problem, whether hidden or subtle or obvious, is feeling like all your troubles are the *fault* of someone else. If it seems that other people are always trying to put you down or push your buttons, you may be a *reactaholic*, with your thoughts, feelings, and behavior totally controlled by whomever or whatever you're reacting to at the moment. The more reactive you are, the more powerless you feel; anger is ultimately a cry of powerlessness.

For example, suppose you're having a bad day at work. Everything is going wrong, and your boss is jumping all over you. You drive home from work in terrible traffic. It's raining; they're playing stupid songs on the radio. You walk in your house to find your kid's toys all over the floor and go berserk. "You lazy, selfish, inconsiderate, little brat, I'm tired of telling you, pick up those toys!"

You can also come home after a great day, feeling pretty good about yourself. You see the shoes in the middle of the floor and say, "Oh, that's just Jimmy or Sally," and not think twice about it. The difference in your reaction to the child's behavior lies entirely within you and depends completely on *how you feel about yourself.*

In the first case the child's behavior seems to devalue your sense of self. "If he cared about me, he wouldn't do this. If my own kid doesn't care about me, I must not be worth caring about." The anger is to punish the child for your devalued sense of self.

In the second instance, the child's behavior does not diminish your sense of personal *importance, value,* and *power.* So there is no *need* for anger. You don't need a tank to solve the problem of the shoe in the middle of the floor. The problem to be solved is how to teach the child to be more considerate; you won't do that by humiliating him because you feel humiliated. His reaction to humiliation will be just the same as yours: an inability to see the other person's perspective and a desire for revenge.

The figure below shows just a few of the dozens of forms of anger. All are no-win attempts to substitute power for value.

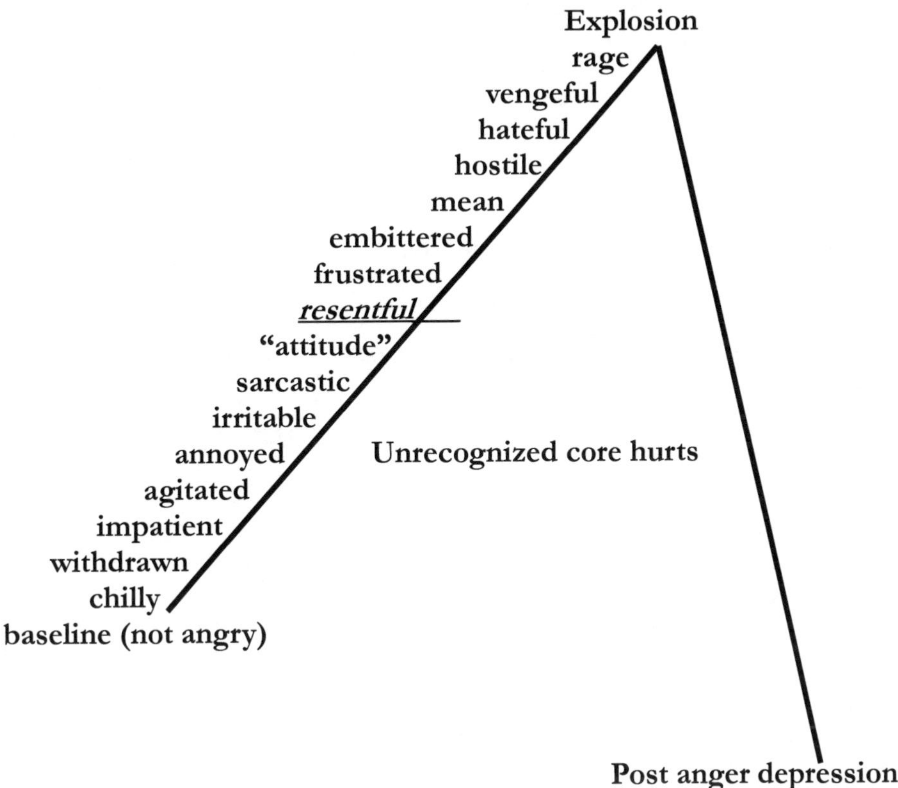

The false power of anger *lasts only as long as the arousal lasts,* and then you feel worse.

Subtle Anger

Our strategy is to build immunity to the low arousal forms of anger at the bottom of the figure, so that the more intense forms do not occur.

The more subtle forms of anger present a couple of special problems. They hardly ever resolve on their own, so they tend to make you feel bad or tired or irritable most of the time. And under stress they quickly escalate to more serious forms of anger. For example, virtually all aggression that is not immediate self-defense or protective of loved ones is preceded by a chain of resentment.

The Anger Arousal Cycle

Physiological component

- Anger comes from a small region of the brain called the limbic system, also known as the mammalian brain, because we share it with all mammals.

- Anger is part of the survival-based fight or flight instinct we share with all mammals.

- Anger mobilizes the organism for one purpose: *fighting.* It's the only emotion that activates *every muscle group and every organ* of the body.

The chemicals secreted in the brain during anger arousal – epinephrine and norepinephrine – feel much like an analgesic and amphetamine – they numb pain and produce a surge of energy. That's how:

- Angry athletes can play with broken bones and not even know about it,
- Wounded animals can be so ferocious.

The experience of threat of physical or psychological pain stimulates the secretion of massive doses of epinephrine and norepinephrine.

As with any amphetamine, once the surge of anger burns out, you *crash*. Anger gives way to some degree of *depression*.

Think about it. The last time you got really angry, you got really depressed, once the amphetamine wore off. The angrier you got, the more depressed you got. And that was merely the physiological response, which occurred even if you kept from doing something while angry that you were ashamed of, like hurting someone you love.

Addictive traps occur when anger is used to escape depressed mood. You get angry, then depressed, then angry again, then depressed again. Pretty soon your brain starts looking for an excuse to get angry just for the energy it brings. This roller coaster ride of energy makes it easy to become an *anger junkie*.

Anger and Health

The ill health effects of anger come not from frequency and intensity – how often you get angry and how angry you get – but from *duration*, how long it lasts. Unhealthy levels of anger are those that last longer than a few minutes.

The anger levels usually present in conflictive relationships give you a 5-7 times greater chance of dying before age 50.

Long lasting levels of anger relate to:

- Destruction of T-Cells (depressing the *immune* system) – if you're angry or resentful often, you probably have lots of little aches and pains, get frequent colds and bouts of flu

- Hypertension (high blood pressure) – increased threat of stroke

- Heart disease

- Cancer

Cognitive (thought) component

Many studies confirm the old saw about being so mad you can't think straight. All levels of anger severely impair thought processes, including:

- Thoughts and judgment

- Reality testing (After being angry, you have to ask someone, "Did that really happen? Did she say that? Did he do that?")

- Perception (We hear and see things inaccurately.)

- Learning and memory (When angry you can recall only things you experienced while you were angry. That's how you can remember a fight with a spouse or the disrespect of a child that happened years ago, yet can't remember any of the sweet and pleasant things they have done since.)

- Problem solving (Don't even try to solve problems when angry or resentful, you'll just make it worse.)

- Creativity (The brain finds creative reasons to stay angry.)

- Performance competence – motor skills deteriorate and error rates escalate. (With the lone exception of hurting someone, *anything* you can do angry, you can do *better* not angry.)

When angry, we misread social cues and mistakenly assume that others are also angry.

Anger polarizes thoughts – you take a more extreme position than you really believe. This makes it difficult to reach any kind of compromise.

Anger causes "thought contraction," a drastic narrowing of the range of thoughts. This makes the person you normally love, who gives meaning to your life, seem like nothing other than a demon who must be punished.

Anger is an attribution of blame – "I feel bad and it's your fault!" The more you blame, the angrier you get, because blame makes you powerless.

Level of Brain Development

Thoughts and language come from the neo cortex, a brain structure unique to humans. You can think of it has the *human* part of the brain, as opposed to the animal part where anger originates.

The neo cortex is not fully developed until age *25*, whereas the capacity for anger is present at birth and has fully developed by age *five*. Anger comes from the *child's* brain; thoughts come from the *adult* brain.

Anger	Thought Regulation
Mammalian **Child**	**Human** **Adult**

In solving a problem in your family, do you want to use your **animal-child** brain or your **human-adult** brain?

Behavioral Component

The goal of angry behavior is to ward off the potential attacker with aggression. All angry animals attempt to:

- Control, neutralize
- Warn, threaten, intimidate (cats arch backs, bulls kick sand, dogs show teeth, humans become tense, rigid, and ready to spring)
- Inflict injury on feelings (confidence, self-esteem, or the ability to resist)
- Inflict injury on body

When angrily arguing about bills, you don't just want to make a point; you want to *control your spouse's decision*, make her back off, or *feel stupid* or *inferior* for not agreeing with you.

Anger provides an immediate surge of energy and numbing of pain – a feeling of physical power – to replace the powerlessness of core hurts.

So if anger works, you're not aware that you're feeling the core hurts. It's the *job* of anger to *numb* pain, so you can attack the *perceived* source of the pain.

While anger numbs the pain of the core hurts, it *prevents* them from *healing*. Anger functions like ice on a wound. As long as you hold ice on a wound, you will not feel pain, and the wound will not heal. Remove the ice and the pain returns. If you use resentment or other low grade anger to numb pain, it will always hurt when you're not angry or resentful.

Consistent anger or resentment makes you more sensitive to core hurts, so that you have to stay angry all the time to protect yourself from the pain. It gives you a low tolerance of and sensitivity to pain. This tends to make you:

- Easily insulted
- Get furious at any kind of criticism
- Always *have* to be "right"

- Demand special consideration (The world owes you!)
- Difficult to get along with at work and home.

Because it focuses attention outside yourself, anger makes you *powerless* to regulate *internal* experience, i.e., core hurts.

Anger and resentment alienate you from your true internal experience, your true thoughts, beliefs, values, and feelings. **This is why the angry you is the not the real you.**

To appreciate the extent that anger renders you powerless over internal experience, consider the picture below, where a man is trying to control his internal experience by controlling his partner's behavior. He wants her to do something to make his core hurts go away.

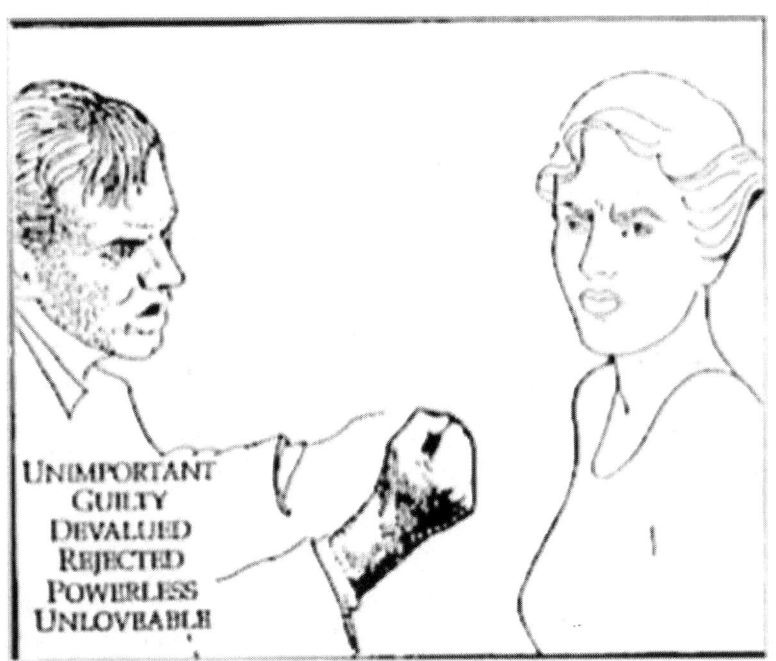

Even if he were married to a saint who would do anything he wanted, a couple of those core hurts would get worse. He would feel guilty, forcing someone he loved to do something she did not want to do. But he would especially feel powerless. His entire sense of self and his ability to regulate his own emotions will depend on her every whim. That would be like relying on your partner to regulate you bladder and tell you when you can go to the bathroom.

The man in the picture below is also trying to control his internal experience by controlling his partner's behavior. Only this time the internal experience is hunger, and he wants her to eat to make his hunger go away.

Of course, this is ridiculous. She can eat until the end of time, and he'll still be hungry. Only *his* behavior (eating) will make his hunger go away.

The same is true of the first picture. Only *he* can regulate his core hurts. The more he wants her to do it for him, the more powerless, frustrated, and angry he becomes.

Holding onto Value under Stress

Two of the hardest things to do in life happen to be crucial to success in relationships:

- **Holding onto self-value when things go badly**
- **Holding onto your value of loved ones when you don't like their behavior.**

These daunting tasks require skill to convert core hurts – and any resentment, anger, or dysfunctional behavior used to numb or avoid them – into self-compassion and compassion for loved ones. In the next session, you will learn how to make this conversion automatic, by mastering a technique called, HEALS™.

SESSION 3: *"Basic Training" of HEALS™*

HEALS™ is a *Core Value* exercise. It builds emotional power, strength, and flexibility by changing core hurts to Core Value. It reduces the power of negative emotions by enhancing Core Value.

The Goal of Practicing HEALS™: is to build a ***skill*** the brain can use ***automatically,*** in a ***fraction*** of a second, to reach **Core Value** when aroused with anger, resentment, anxiety, or obsessions.

Just like basic training in the military, it takes lots of practice to develop a skill that will work ***automatically*** **under stress.** The key is making the skill part of your automatic response to stress.

It takes an average of **six weeks** of **12 repetitions per day,** ***associated*** with ***imagined*** or ***recalled*** **anger** or **anxiety** arousal, for the skill to become ***automatic.***

How the Technology Works

HEALS™ lowers baseline resentment in the stream of unconscious everyday emotions. With your level of resentment lowered, any waves of negative emotion will be less intense, less likely to do harm, and more likely to motivate behavior that heals, corrects, and improves. With your overall resentment levels lowered, you will once again experience interest and enjoyment.

HEALS™ does not make you "suppress" or "keep the lid on" or "put up with it" or "ignore it" or "hold it in." Far from making you tolerate discomfort, HEALS™ *changes* the painful emotion automatically, just like a thermostat automatically changes the room temperature from uncomfortable to comfortable. HEALS™ moves you from a devaluing state to a valuing one, from core hurts to Core Value.

Like all skill acquisition, mastering HEALS™ is hard at first but gets much easier with practice. It took you a long time to learn how to drive, but now you do it without thinking. The same was true of learning to ride a bike. As you master HEALS™ you will reap the reward of rising self-esteem and well being, with diminishing effort, as the figure below indicates.

The Effort and Reward of Learning HEALS™

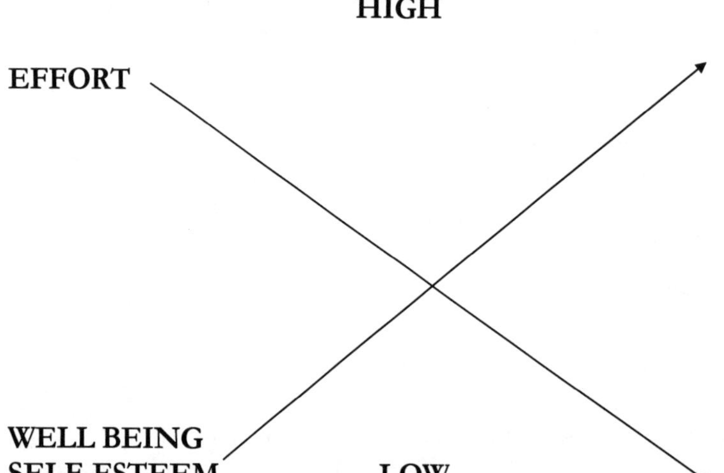

Practice Time: Beginning 2 weeks 4 weeks 6 weeks

Practicing HEALS™

Remember, you are practicing HEALS™ to build a *future* skill that will automatically regulate anger, resentment, and anxiety. In the interest of discipline, it is best to establish a practice-routine of regular repetitions for the next six weeks. The suggested regimen below covers transitional times, which are the most likely to produce negative emotions.

- Once before you get out of bed – this is the most important repetition, as it will start your stream of unconscious everyday emotions *positively*.
- Once before you leave the house,
- Once before you go to work,
- Once at morning break time,
- Once at lunch time,
- Once at afternoon break time,
- Once before you leave work,
- Once before you go into the house,
- Once before dinner,
- Once after dinner,
- Once while preparing for bed,
- Once in bed.

There are *no bad times or places* to practice HEALS™. However, for maximum positive effect on you stream of unconscious emotions, do not practice it twice in a row.

The Steps of HEALS™

HEALS, HEALS, HEALS flashes in your imagination
Experience the ***deepest* core hurt** (inadequate/unlovable)
Access **Core Value Bank**

Basic Humanity	Meaning & Purpose	Love	Spiritual
The emotions I felt as I imagined rescuing and comforting the desperate child:	The most important thing about me as a person: The most important thing about my life in general:	The people I love:	My spiritual connection:
Nature	**Creativity**	**Community**	**Compassion**
Something beautiful in nature:	Something beautiful human made (art, music, architecture, furniture, etc.):	My community connection:	Compassionate things I have done: 1. 2. 3.

Love yourself by feeling compassion for other person's core hurt (inadequate/unlovable)
Solve the problem

Start each practice repetition by recalling a time when you felt disregarded, ignored, accused, devalued, or disrespected. (For the first two weeks, start with relatively mild provocation. As with any skill, you should start small – you learn to swim in shallow water, not in the ocean during a storm. For the first three weeks stay away from the more complex forms of anger like jealousy and disputes about raising your children. HEALS™ works on this kind of layered anger, but it requires about three-four weeks of practice time.

- Imagine the incident in as much detail as you can.
- Pretend it's happening *now*.
- Feel the tightness in your neck, eyes, jaw, shoulders, chest, stomach, and hands.
- Do anger self-talk:

"It's not fair, they shouldn't be doing this, it isn't right! I'll show them!"

"Here we go again!"
"It'll never stop!"
"They always do this!"

As soon as you feel the anger: "**HEALS**" suddenly flashes in your imagination. (See the word flashing and hear the sound of it.)

HEALS…HEALS…HEALS…

Feel yourself move downward to your Core Value.

Experience the *deepest* core hurt *causing* the resentment or anger. Say,

"I am powerless, I am unlovable."

Have the courage to deeply feel, for just *one second*, what it's like to *be* that core hurt. Feel what it's like to be completely powerless and unworthy, something like, "I'm a puppet on a string. They control everything I think, feel, and do." Or, "No one could ever pay attention to my opinions or feelings. I don't count. No one could love the *real* me."

Access the glow of *Core Value,* the most important part of you, the part of you that would rescue a child in desert. Invoke the emotions of your Core Value Bank. You have the *power* to act in your best interest, regardless of what anyone else does. Feel your Core Value grow.

Love yourself by feeling compassion. Prove, beyond a doubt, how powerful and worthy you are; recognize the Core Value of the person who offended you. That person has a Core Value Bank like yours and would rescue the child in the desert like you would. Feel compassion for the core hurt that has disconnected that person from Core Value. It's almost always the same one you felt. Recognize that person's Core Value, and yours will soar.

Solve the problem in your best interest.

After each repetition, ask yourself:
"Will I solve this better (in my long-term best interests) from my Core Value or with anger?
Which do I prefer?
Which is more authentically me?

Each repetition of HEALS™ makes your emotional system stronger and more flexible, just as each push-up makes your skeletal-muscular system stronger and more flexible. But just as with push-ups, it takes a lot of repetitions for it go get really strong and flexible.

Each time you practice HEALS™, you gain a little more of your inner self. You become wiser, more powerful, and better able to understand yourself and others.

The Vaccination Effect of HEALS™

When you receive vaccination against a virus or bacterium such as diphtheria, measles, or TB, you are injected with a small, non-toxic dose of the disease. This stimulates your immune system to build immunity against the illness. In the same way, your brief experience of the deepest core hurt with each practice repetition of HEALS™ works like a vaccination. It will build immunity to core hurts so that no one will be able to push your buttons or make you act against your best interests.

Path of HEALS™

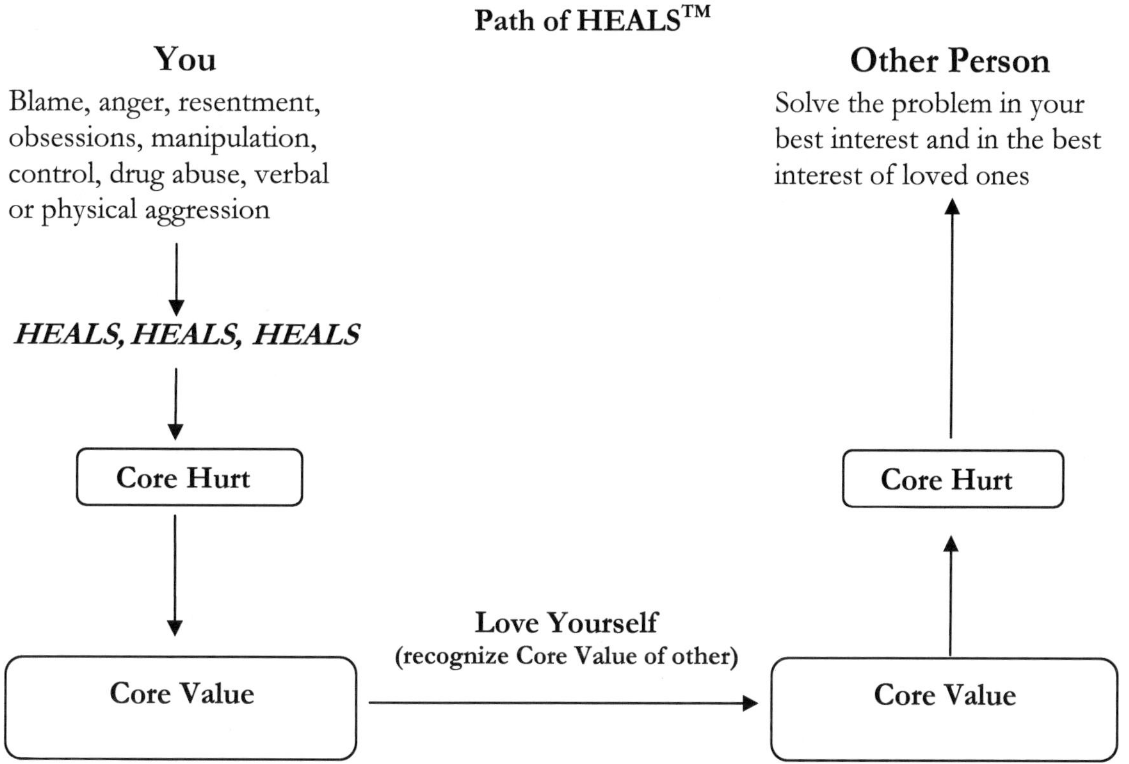

The Emotional Wave

The major problem most people encounter when they first start practicing HEALS™ is trying to experience the emotion while "remembering" the steps *and* the incident. There are audio tapes and a CD-ROM available to help you learn the steps (compassionpower.com). After about three weeks of practice, awareness of the steps should fall away completely. You will experience a purely emotional wave, going from resentment, anger, anxiety, or obsessions, quickly through core hurts to Core Value, to solving the problem with self value and value for others. The emotional wave will be *without thought*, but it might be labeled:

***HEALS* flashing**
Core hurt
Core Value
Love (compassion)
Solve the problem

By the end of your work with HEALS™, you will be so focused on making the situation better that you won't notice the automatic transition from resentment/anger to Core Value.

Directions for the "Experience" Step of HEALS™

Always go to the *deepest* core hurt. HEALS™ will not work if you do not go deeply enough. If the core hurt is "rejection" and you identify "unimportant," you have not validated your true emotional experience. That unregulated core hurt will cause more resentment and anger.

However, HEALS™ *will* work if you go "too deep." If the core hurt is "unimportant," and you identify "unlovable," regulation will still occur.

Disregarded: Feel what it's like to feel unworthy of regard, not to count enough for anyone to pay attention to your opinions, desires, and emotions.

Unimportant: Feel what it's like to be totally unimportant, not to matter at all, to be so unimportant that no one should consider having a passing positive thought about you.

Accused/Guilty: Feel what it is like to have done something wrong, to have hurt someone, to have done terrible damage, to have betrayed someone, to have been immoral.

Devalued: Feel what it's like to be totally without value as a person. You are *worthless*.

Rejected: Feel what it's like to be completely unacceptable, banished, put down, thrown out, or abandoned.

Powerless: Feel what it's like to be completely without power over your internal experience, to be out of control of your thoughts and emotions. You're like a puppet on a string or a robot whose buttons anyone can push. Anybody can make you think, feel, and do anything they want.

Unlovable: Feel what it's like to be unworthy of love. No one could love you. No one could love the real you. No one ever will.

Trouble with HEALS™

If you have trouble with HEALS™, try the following:

1. Go deeper on the core hurt list. Don't be afraid to feel "inadequate or unlovable," even if it seems worse than the core hurt you actually felt. Try to get as close as you can to feeling the *deepest* core hurt for one second.

2. If you have trouble making the transition to Core Value, try rapid eye movement. Focus your eyes on your finger and move it rapidly back and forth a few seconds.

3. In the "Access Core Value" step, deeply appreciate that, no matter what the trigger incident, you do not deserve to continue feeling core hurts. Continuing to feel core hurts *impedes* your ability to make things better.

4. In the "Love yourself" step, recognize the Core Value of the person who offended you. He/she is far more complicated, complex, and humane than whatever he or she did to you. Appreciating the complexity of other people reinforces your own.

5. In the "Love yourself" step, identify the other person's core hurt that caused the behavior you don't like. (It will almost always be the same one you felt.) Feel compassion, not for the behavior, but for the hurt.

SESSION 4: *Practice HEALS™*

Spend two hours practicing **HEALS™**.

SESSION 5: *The Success of Everything*

Are there any problems with **HEALS™**?

The success of everything that follows in this course depends on developing the *conditioned* Core Value reflex that **HEALS™** provides. Successful completion of the course *requires* mastery of **HEALS™**. Anyone who needs individual help should ask.

There will be spot checks to see if participants can complete the exercise out loud, in *less than a minute*. Failure to do so will mean the **HEALS™** sessions must be repeated.

Compassion as Defense

Compassion is the best psychological defense you can have. It's the most effective way to prevent hurt in that it:

- Restores Core Value, which takes away the ability of other people to hurt you emotionally

- Rarely stimulates anger in others, making hostile or destructive defenses *unnecessary*

- Offers superior protection from the pain of betrayed trust. **No one has felt hurt due to compassion, although many people have been harmed by *unwise trust*.** Compassion makes us *less likely* to trust unwisely, as it provides deeper understanding of the danger presented by those unable to regulate core hurts.

We can never feel taken advantage of or exploited in the experience of compassion, for compassion is its own reward. Even if it turns out that someone else's defenses or weaknesses have motivated manipulation, we have the self-satisfaction of knowing that we acted out of compassion, which is always the right thing.

Note: Compassion for others is an *easy* step from self-compassion. Any trouble at all feeling compassion for others signifies the need for more self-compassion.

Compassion and Disagreement

Compassion requires validation of and sympathy with the emotions of another, *regardless* of disagreement about the thoughts, beliefs, or ideas that go with the emotions. In other words, you can disagree 24-7 and still have compassion for your loved ones.

In the event of disagreement, you must make a *sincere* effort to understand the importance of the beliefs, goals, and desires of your partner or child, *and* to sympathize with any disappointment if the desire cannot be met. If you fail at compassion, resolution of the disagreement becomes virtually impossible. Compassion does not always make it better, but failure of compassion always makes it worse.

Problem:

> Your children do not receive this compassion training, so they do not know how to value and sympathize with emotions that result from disagreements. **They need you to *model* the method for them, to *teach* them compassion.**
>
> **Compassion tends to stimulate compassion in loved ones, almost as surely as anger stimulates anger.**

If you feel devalued by something your partner, child, or parent says or does, he or she probably feels devalued too. **Devaluing him or her in return will only make it *worse*.** Compassion will make it *better*.

Compassion v. "Giving in"

Compassion does not mean giving in. Giving in or "going along to avoid an argument" virtually guarantees resentment. Resentment undermines and ruins attachment relationships.

Most of the time resolution without resentment is possible with a sincere effort to *understand* one another. We become the angriest (the most hurt), not when disappointed for not getting what we want, but when feeling *misunderstood* or *disregarded*. With compassion, we *never* feel unimportant or disregarded or unlovable (although we may feel disappointed). This makes negotiation on all issues much easier. Compassion is absolutely *necessary* for resolution in the event of hurt feelings.

Example:

> Not getting this new car or that new wardrobe does not mean that you do not deserve it. You *do* deserve it, and I am sorry that we can't get it for you. This is *why* we can't get it....

Understanding brings the parties of a dispute closer, while anger drives them further apart.

Compassion does not necessarily include generosity or magnanimity. It requires that we understand and regard the feelings of others as *vital factors* but not the *only factors* in decisions.

With compassion we avoid the leading cause of death of attachment relationships: **Power Struggles**. With compassion the goal is not to "win" a dispute, but to find a solution in which *all* parties feel regarded, important, and valuable.

COMPASSION *NEVER* MEANS TOLERATING ABUSE

Compassion helps explain unacceptable behavior, but it also requires that unacceptable behavior *change* and that abusive behavior *stop immediately*, for the sake of everyone in the family. It is not compassionate to allow someone to indulge in the self-destruction of abusing a loved one.

Failures of Compassion: Definitions of Abuse

Abuse is hurting the feelings or body of someone else to alter some unpleasant feeling within the self. Because compassion regulates unpleasant internal feelings, all abuse is a *failure of compassion.*

Physical abuse: Hitting, punching, slapping, pushing, grabbing, kicking, and any unwanted touching, sexual or non-sexual, as well as threatening, coercing, or intimidating.

Emotional abuse: Attacks on **autonomy, identity, privacy, sense of self, or self-esteem; attempting to control, isolate, or force behavior against his or her will.** Criticizing **what a person *is***, rather than what he/she *does.*

Abusive	Non-Abusive
"You're lazy."	"I feel you can do a little more to help keep the house clean."
"You're stupid."	"I disagree with your opinion."
"You're a slut."	"I felt jealous when I saw you talk to him. I need to regulate my jealousy."
"You're a bitch."	"I feel bad when you shout."
"You're a bad kid."	"I don't like it when you talk disrespectfully to me."

This form of abuse is called "negative labeling." Besides the fact that it's abusive, the use of negative labels virtually guarantees that you'll get more of the negative behavior you're describing. After all, what do "lazy" people do? Well, they don't help around the house, for one thing. What do "bad" kids do?

The Anger-Junkie's Constant Song: "Justifying Anger Blues"

Anger, the most potentially destructive and dangerous of emotions, is also the most socially inhibited. The gravest laws in civilized society seek to stop anger-driven behavior.

Anger is socially acceptable only when mitigating circumstances justify it. So the anger-addicted brain (in need of epinephrine and norepinephrine for energy and relief of pain), constantly seeks **justification** of anger, **ignoring all contrary evidence** in the process.

When the brain needs a jolt of epinephrine and norepinephrine, *judgment and reasoning greatly suffer.* The lust to see only those possibilities that justify anger guarantees failure to comprehend most relevant possibilities. That's why anger-junkies justifying their anger sound like alcoholics trying to justify their drinking by suggesting that alcohol has nutritional value.

Regardless of personal levels of intelligence, **during anger arousal** we generally perform as if we have a **thought disorder** or **learning disability**.

The most common thought distortions that occur during anger arousal:

- "I'm the victim"
- all-or-nothing thinking (no shades of gray)
- polarized thinking – taking a position more extreme or even contrary to actual beliefs
- ego-centralizing – can see no one else's point of view
- catastrophizing – "This is *terrible*," no matter how trivial it actually is
- over-generalizing – if everybody did the trivial thing, the world would be horrible; or this *always* happens, you *always* do that, you *never* do this
- paranoia – everyone's trying to make you feel bad
- mental processing errors:
    - misreading social cues – supposing that others feel the same way you do
    - visual processing – don't see what's actually there, or see things that aren't actually there
    - auditory processing – can't hear what is actually said or imagine you hear something different
    - reading comprehension
    - emotional numbing – out of touch with all emotions or with all emotions except anger.

General Rule: **If you have to justify your emotions or behavior, to yourself or others, they are almost always *harmful.***

The urge to justify should be a trigger to **heal the hurt that causes the anger**. Justifying anger *never* heals the hurt that causes it.

Are You an Anger-Junkie?

You may be an *anger junkie* if you use anger:

- for energy or motivation (can't get going or keep going without some degree of anger)
- pain relief (it hurts when you're not angry)
- confidence, a stronger sense of self – you only feel certain when angry
- to avoid depression
- to enforce a sense of entitlement (people *owe* you)
- to inhibit or punish disagreement with your opinions and values
- more than once a day and it lasts for more than a few minutes.

The cure for anger addiction is compassion for self and loved ones and *regular practice of* HEALS™.

Normal Negative Feelings + Core Hurts + Blame = Anger

Disappointment, sadness, anxiety, and **distress** are part of everyday living. Only if they stimulate *core hurts* that are *blamed* on someone will they become anger.

Disappointment means you didn't get something you wanted. It doesn't mean that you are unworthy of it, it just means you didn't get it.

Sadness means you've lost something. It doesn't mean that you are unlovable, it just means that you lost something.

Anxiety is a dread that something bad might happen. It does not tell you that *you* are bad; it tells you to pay attention to a problem, so you can *solve* it.

Distress means that you are currently overloaded in emotional response. It doesn't mean that you are inadequate; it means your overexcited emotional circuits need a moment to calm. HEALS™ will do the trick quickly.

Jealousy is a dramatic example of an ordinary emotion that becomes a problem when it stimulates a cycle of core hurts and blame. When that happens, jealousy becomes obsessional, which can make you psychotic.

The hidden meaning of pathological jealousy is, "I'm not lovable, so she must want someone else."

If deep in our hearts we feel that we are not worthy of love or cannot sustain love and compassion for others, we will not believe those who say they love us. They either love the false self or they want something or someone else.

The more we try to manage jealousy by swallowing it or by attempting to control the behavior of others, the more powerless over it we grow.

Once jealousy stimulates core hurts, it becomes, like all anger, a signal to increase Core Value. With Core Value restored, you can carry out the *natural* function of jealousy.

The natural function of jealousy in relationships is to warn of emotional distance. The only thing that relieves the pain of jealousy is for you to be more compassionate and loving. If you are, you will likely close the distance between you and your loved one and eliminate jealousy. If you are not compassionate and loving, the distance will widen and you will get more and more jealous and do greater damage to yourself and to your relationships.

Jealousy Eradicator

1. Restore Core Value
2. Be more compassionate and loving.

Anger, Violence, and Masculinity

The following quizzes point out the true nature of anger and violence in terms of adult masculinity.

Please identify the family member to whom the question most likely refers. Write your answers before looking below.

1. Who are the most violent people in the vast majority of families?

2. This family member most often uses anger as a defense.

3. If this family member doesn't get his/her own way, violence is likely.

4. If hurt or offended, this family member wants to hit or throw something.

The correct answer for each question is: *a child under three.* The trick is when we hear "violence" we think "damage." Toddlers do no damage with their violence and mean no ill-will, so we tend not to think of their behavior as *violence.* The point is that the impulse to anger and aggression is not manly. It's not even adult; it's *childish.* It comes from the child's brain, and needs to be regulated by the adult brain.

The Wimp Test

Why We Need to Grow Beyond Gender Stereotypes

Write **REAL MAN** next to those statements you think describe someone of courage, or **WIMP** next to those statements you think describe a wimp.

1. He's afraid to be honest.
2. He won't admit to himself what he really feels.
3. He's afraid to take responsibility for himself and blames others for what he thinks, feels, and does.
4. He's afraid to feel like an adult and give up the defenses of a two year-old.
5. He can't feel good about himself unless he feels better than someone else.
6. He's afraid to be intimate.
7. He's afraid to be compassionate.
8. He hides behind anger, because he's afraid to feel core hurts.
9. Is a real man *afraid* to feel hurt? Does he *need* to cover up his feelings with anger and violence?
10. Would a real man hurt a woman or a child to keep from feeling a few seconds of rejection, or disrespect, or devaluation?"

The Wimp Test reframes traditional macho values in terms of *fear*. This highlights the contraction in cultural definitions of masculinity. Most cultures describe manliness as *courage*, the ability to withstand pain and overcome fear to protect what you most value. Yet popular images of masculinity often imply terror of your own emotions. The Marlboro Man rides alone into the desert to smoke himself to death, because speaking to a woman might cause an emotion he won't be able to handle. Talk about powerlessness!

Real power comes from the courage to face any emotion and regulate those that lead to self-destructive behavior, especially hurting people you love.

Real power is compassion.

SESSION 6: *Foundation of Genuine Self-Esteem*

Realistic self-esteem is the immune system of the self. It helps keep us psychologically fit and tells us when our health is in decline. The better we feel about ourselves, the better we handle stress, anxiety, anger, rejection, love, and joy. The better we feel about ourselves, the better we do in life.

Self-esteem is a form of **pride** that includes motivation to do something. It provides **morale** or the **spirit to go on.**

Hurtful, conflictive, or abusive relationships wreak havoc on the self-esteem of everyone in the family. However, the effects may be subtle, due to an adaptive, **false self-esteem** that keeps the parties going, however painfully, under the stress of conflict and abuse.

Elements of Genuine Self-esteem

Research on people with high self-esteem has shown that they:

- Have skill in self-regulation (They don't often get angry.)
- Continually learn and acquire new skills or deepen old skills (They don't "stand pat.")
- Do what they sincerely believe to be the "right thing"
- Maintain flexibility to look at situations from various perspectives
- Respect and value themselves and others.

In contrast, people with low self-esteem:

- Blame others for their emotions and behavior (makes them powerless)
- Tend to be aggressive or overly passive (not assertive)
- Rely on the response of others to feel good about themselves
- Suffer narrow and rigid points of view (only one "right way" to do things)
- Suffer jealousy and envy.

The Golden Rule of Self-Esteem

THE ROAD TO PSYCHOLOGICAL **RUIN** BEGINS WITH **BLAME**.
THE ROAD TO PSYCHOLOGICAL **POWER** BEGINS WITH **RESPONSIBILITY**.

Blame v. Responsibility

***You cannot blame and find good solutions at the same time.* You must choose between blame and making things better.**

Blame comes from the limbic system or *child* brain. (Toddlers blame because they don't know how to solve problems.) **Solutions** must come from the *thinking* or *adult* brain.

Blame is always about the **past**. Solutions must occur in the **present** and **future**.

Blame obscures solutions by locking your focus on how bad the problem seems or how bad someone else is for causing it.

Blame focuses attention on damage, injury, defects, weakness - on what is *wrong*. Blame makes you feel like a **powerless** victim.

THE ROAD TO *POWER* BEGINS WITH *RESPONSIBILITY*.

Responsibility focuses attention on strengths, resiliency, competence, growth, creativity, healing, and compassion, all of which are necessary for solving family problems.

Example: Someone plows into my car parked legally on the street. That's not my fault. But it's my responsibility to get it fixed. As long as I **blame** the hit-and-run driver for the expense and inconvenience of the accident, I experience anger, anxiety, and helplessness. It becomes later and darker, and I'm not going anywhere.

But as I assume **responsibility** for the repairs, I *empower* myself to find another means of transportation. In addition, I am:

- Doing the right thing in the circumstance
- Regulating anxiety and anger that diminish self-esteem
- Giving myself a jolt of self-esteem.

I *reward* myself for acting responsibly. Now getting my car fixed becomes an "injection" of self-esteem, rather than a blast of shame and anger. I take pleasure in my resourcefulness.

Hierarchical Self-Esteem: No Way to Win

Persons with hierarchical self-esteem need to feel better than someone else to feel okay about themselves. They view people in terms of **superiority** and **inferiority**. Not surprisingly, this form of distorted self-esteem lies at the heart of racism, sexism, and all other prejudicial points of view.

The most abusive form of hierarchical self-esteem is **predatory self-esteem**. To feel good about themselves, persons with predatory self-esteem need to *make* other people feel bad about themselves.

The most frequent victims or predators are members of their own families. Many family abusers in therapy test high in self-esteem, while everyone else in the family tests low. When intervention increases the self-esteem of the emotionally beaten-down spouse and children, the predator's self-esteem always *declines*.

Predatory self-esteem is always false self-esteem, rising on a wave of criticism used to put down loved ones. When arousal wears off or when victims no longer internalize the criticism, the predator drops once again into depression, with the added burden of shame for having hurt loved ones.

Hierarchical self-esteem is a virtually unachievable goal. You will always meet people superior to you. You will always meet persons who are smarter, wealthier, more powerful, better looking, more popular, and so on; failure is the inevitable end of this precarious notion of self-worth.

Lateral Self-Esteem: The Power of Equality

A no-lose approach to self-esteem invokes the **power of equality**. If you believe in the essential equality of all people, you will never meet anyone better than you. A steady supply of self-esteem comes from efforts to increase other people's self-esteem, by treating them, without regard to station or status, with dignity and respect. The royal road to self-regard and self-empowerment passes through regard and empowerment of others.

It takes far more power to help loved ones build their self-esteem than to criticize, attack, humiliate, or tear down their self-esteem.

False (superficial) Pride

False Pride afflicts those with:

- Hierarchical or predatory self-esteem
- Exclusively external measures of self-esteem (what other people think), with no personal values or conviction base
- Investment of pride in merely one or two aspects of the self, while disowning other crucial qualities or shrouding them in shame.

False pride requires self-obsession to maintain. Those who suffer from it must continually manipulate others to keep the illusion going. They violate their most human need: to experience genuine compassion.

Examples of false pride:

- The Nazis were competent and creative without being compassionate.

- Many physicians are competent and creative, without being nurturing or compassionate. (Research shows hat they have a lower cure rate than their less knowledgeable but more compassionate colleagues.)

- Many people are nurturing without being competent or truly compassionate, which involves understanding deeper needs and long-term best interests. For instance, it's not compassionate to give an alcoholic a drink or to give children everything they want.

Genuine pride is pride in oneself as a **competent, creative, growth-oriented, nurturing, compassionate** person.

Compassion is the most fertile wellspring of **genuine pride** and **genuine self-esteem**.

How to Tell Genuine Pride from False Pride

People with **False Pride** fear humiliation. They use anger, alcohol, drugs, workaholism, etc. to avoid humiliation. They use *force* to punish embarrassment or perceived humiliation.

People with **Genuine Pride** *never* feel humiliated by the behavior of others. Other people can embarrass them only for a few seconds, before self-regulation occurs. The behavior of no one but the self can diminish the sense of self.

SESSION 7: *Power Struggles*

More than anything else, power struggles destroy the self-building quality of attachment. Once again, the elements of self-building in attachment relationships:

1. **Unconditional safety and security for all parties;**
2. **High levels of compassion;**
3. **Freedom from resentment, hostility, abuse, and other emotional constraints.**

If an attachment relationship consistently fails in any of the above, it loses its self-building function and does more harm than good. If it falls below the threshold of safety and security, it becomes **self-destroying**.

Power struggles happen when people contend with one another to avoid feeling powerless. Failing to internally regulate powerless feelings, they try to force each other to *submit.* "Triumph" over the other provides *temporary* relief of powerlessness. Power struggles *always* result in more **resentment** and **hostility**.

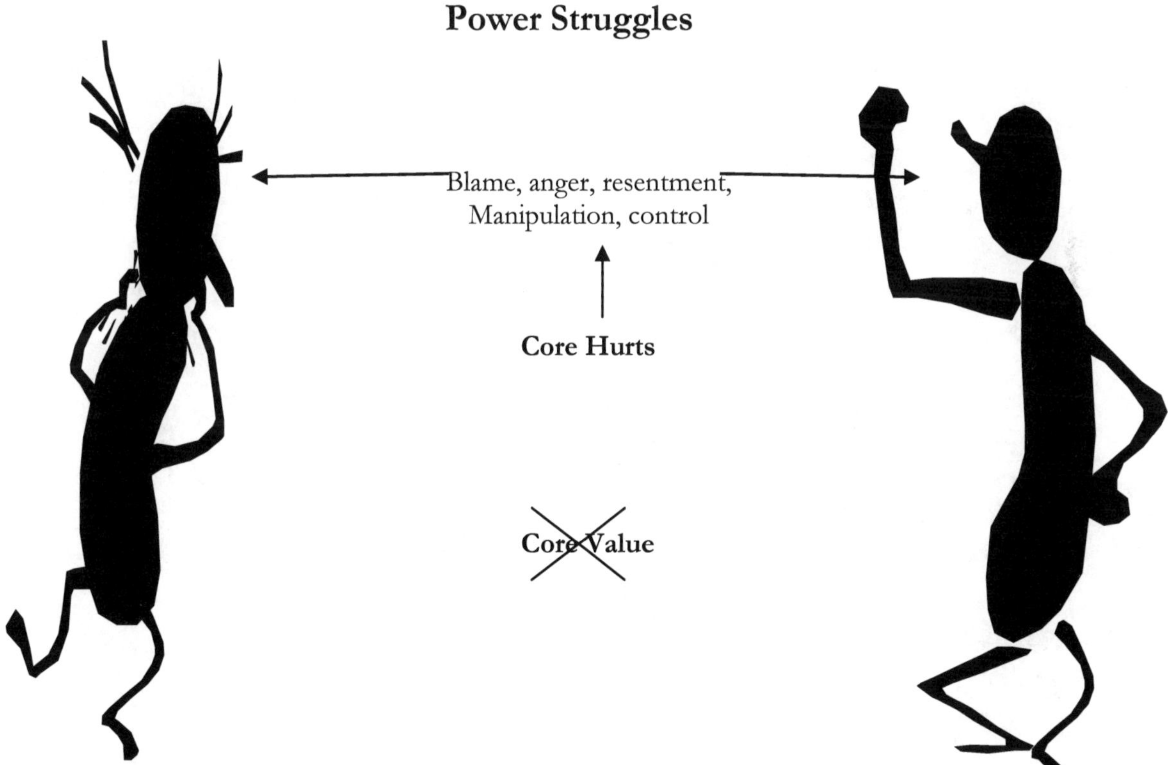

Non-abusive power can occur only in a context of *responsibility*, which necessarily includes respect for the rights and feelings of others. The more *power* you have, the more *responsibility* you must accept.

Power Struggle Facts

When one person wins, everybody loses.

You cannot diminish or hurt people you love without diminishing and hurting yourself.

You cannot enhance and empower your spouse or children without enhancing and empowering you.

You cannot diminish or hurt the parent of your children without diminishing and hurting your children.

Note: it is extremely harmful to children to say negative things about their parents, even if you think they are true. Children identify with both of their parents and are likely to hate the qualities in themselves that they identify with the ridiculed parent.

Power Struggle Quiz I

1. To make myself feel valuable, I

a. become angry
b. try to control my loved ones
c. value my loved ones and myself

2. To make myself feel above accusation, I

a. become angry
b. accuse back
c. try to find a solution to the problem causing the accusation

3. To make myself feel acceptable, I

a. become angry
b. reject them before they can reject me
c. force them not to reject me
d. refuse to reject myself

4. To make myself feel powerful, I

a. become angry
b. try to control my loved ones
c. empower my loved ones to find solutions that make everyone feel important and valuable

5. To make myself feel lovable, I

a. become angry
b. feel compassion for myself and my loved ones
c. allow myself to love
d. show my love

Power Struggle Quiz II

Which gives you more power?

a) Winning a dispute
b) Resolving a dispute in such a way that all parties feel the best they can feel

2. You cannot win, if someone you love loses.

a) True
b) False

3. Which gives you more power?

a) Dominating your spouse or children
b) Empowering your spouse or children

4. Do you empower your loved ones by:

a) Telling them what to do (or not to do)
b) Helping them come up with a solution

5. What is genuine personal power?

a) Power over your internal experience
b) The ability to bully, intimidate, or use force against a spouse or child

6. What motivates a person to control someone else?

a) Fear of a mistake?
b) Fear of chaos?
c) Fear of feeling something he or she doesn't want to feel?
d) Irrational belief that there's only one right way to do things.
e) All the above.

Note: The fears embodied in question number six are *internal.* They require *internal regulation.* Exerting power and control over loved ones only makes these fears *worse*, leading eventually to outright *paranoia*, while destroying trust and creating an atmosphere of resentment and hostility.

Laws of Human Nature in Relationships

(Keep this page handy so you can identify which level you are on and to which you must move.)

When disputes occur on the level of symptoms and defenses, the problem cannot be solved *until* each party:

- Acknowledges the core hurts of self and loved ones;
- Activates Core Value;
- Supports loved ones to access their Core Value.

In other words, once anger and resentment get triggered, do **HEALS™** before getting into the specifics of the problem.

The Secret of Avoiding Power Struggles

A mode of self is a way or style of thinking, feeling, and behaving. When in a certain mode of self, your brain chooses from a pre-set selection of thoughts, feelings, and behavior, based on past experience.

Every adult human being has **Weak Modes** of self as well as **Power Modes** of Self.

WEAK MODES	POWER MODES
Helpless	**Competent**
Dependent	**Growth/Creative**
Depressive	**Healing/Nurturing**
Destructive	**Compassionate**

In trying to settle disputes with parents, spouses, and children, which modes of self do you want to activate? Of course you want Power Modes – you'll just make things worse in a weak mode.

Now here's the trick, which mode of self do you want to activate in your loved one? Of course you want them to be in Power Modes too, because things can only get worse if they stay in weak modes. Yet power struggle tactics, including all forms of anger and resentment, are designed to put the other person in a weak mode. That is why things always deteriorate in power struggles.

To avoid power struggles, you have to think *empowerment*, which means putting your loved ones and yourself in Power Modes.

First we'll see how to empower children and then adults.

Core Value Parenting:
Empower Children to Behave, Grow, and Achieve their Potential

It is more dangerous to be a child now than ever before in human history. Children face much higher risks to safety than at any non-war period of history. Common challenges include the threat of violence, drugs, STDs, pregnancy, auto crashes, and suicide.

More children are murdered and assaulted by adults and other children than ever before in the history of the world.

They experience much greater anxiety from far more choices about things like appearance, food, drink, behavior, peers, leisure activities, studies, and their future.

At a time when they need more emotional connection, adult supervision, and community support, they have far less of these things than at any other point of human history.

According to research, children believe that their parents love them but do not *value* them. They do not feel important to their parents, whom they see as *burdened* by parental love. Why do they feel that way?

The biggest complaints of children of all ages about their parents are **yelling** and **not listening.** Listening to children and speaking respectfully to them makes them feel valued.

The greatest leverage parents have to help and guide children is to form strong, resentment-free emotional bonds with them, based on value, mutual respect, and *empowerment.*

Empowerment gives someone the right and the confidence to offer solutions to problems that respect the best interests of all involved. In other words, it activates Core Value and motivations to improve, appreciate, connect, and protect.

The trick in empowering children is to get them to come up with solutions that work for them *and* you. When *they* come up with the solutions, you avoid power struggles, resentment, and hostility. Most people, including children, like to *cooperate* but hate to *submit.*

The ultimate goals of empowerment are:

1. Teach the *Five R's* of Parenting (and successful living):
   - ◊ **Resourcefulness** (problem solving and creativity)
   - ◊ **Responsibility**
   - ◊ **Respect**
   - ◊ **Relationship investment** (respect for the emotions of other people)
   - ◊ **Regulation of impulses and emotions**

2. Channel the child's intelligence and creativity into solving the problem, *in consideration of other people's rights*, rather than opposing or resenting your solution

3. Teach negotiation skills

4. Model compassion

5. Teach morality (arbitrarily exerting power and control over others is wrong).

6. **Protect them from the negative influence of peers.** (Research shows that negative influence of peers is the biggest single facture leading to the failure and harm of children. When parents have good relationships with their children, peers have less negative influence.)

Making Choices w*ithin* Natural, Legal & Social Limitations

Children develop self-esteem, problem-solving skills, and compassion when they make choices within clearly defined limits set by parents. Think of parental limits as a box that contains choices and solutions for children to make. With young children, the box is narrow. As they grow in problem-solving skill and respect for the rights of others, the box of choices and solutions grows larger.

Limits Set by Parental Authority

Parental Authority	**Choices, Solutions: Ages 2-5**	Parental Authority

Parental Authority

The box below shows areas in which older children can make limited choices. Once again, the limits set by parents *widen* as the children mature and develop responsibility and respect for the rights of others. If they behave *responsibly*, the box *grows*. If they behave *irresponsibly*, the box *shrinks*. Thus children learn a most valuable lesion in life: responsibility goes hand-in-hand with power and privilege. Within this framework, they understand that *their* behavior – not your moods or "power trips" – entirely controls the amount of power and responsibility they enjoy.

Limits Set by Parental Authority

Parental Authority	**Choices, Solutions: 6-18** Privileges Responsibilities Chores/duties Personal appearance Rewards Sanctions Spending allowance, money gifts	Parental Authority

Parental Authority

Negotiation/Cooperation

The most crucial skill for success in work, school, and relationships is the ability to negotiate and cooperate.

Cooperation (Teamwork):

- Willing (not necessarily *preferred*) participation in work, problem solving, or task-accomplishment

- Gives everyone equal respect, regardless of unequal gifts, talents, resources, etc.

- Acknowledges the equal rights of everyone

- Gives **freedom of choice**, *so long as the choice violates no agreements* and *encroaches on no one's boundaries.*

Negotiation:

- Is the attempt to bring about cooperative behavior
- Requires far more intelligence, skill, and responsibility than dominance or submission
- Can never be threatening, punishing, or shaming.

Setting up the Empowerment Model of Parenting

At first children may not trust the empowerment model. Older children may see it as another form of power struggle. To gain their trust, it is best to set up the model at the same time that you establish a **formal family meeting.** The meeting should be once week, at regular times, limited to 20 minutes.

Even if the children resist at first, keep the model in place for at least three weeks. By that time they should see that it works much better for them and for you.

Begin the meeting by reading the following. Each family member should read a bullet. Keep passing the agreement around until you are finished.

Empowerment Agreement

We hereby agree that our connection as a family is important and valuable to us. We care about each other and want the best for one another. We acknowledge that each individual in the family:

- Is a separate person, important, valuable, and lovable in his/her own right;

- Has the right to grow and develop fully and to realize his/her fullest potential;

- Has needs, desires, and preferences that will sometimes conflict with those of other members of the family;

- Has the right to come up with solutions to problems that consider the rights, needs, desires, and preferences of other family members and that fall within safety, health, and growth guidelines set by parents and the law;

- Agrees to negotiate respectfully with other members of the family, without resorting to the use of power, control, or violence.

Accordingly, we agree to:

- State our problems clearly and specifically, *without blame;*

- Try to think of more than one solution for each problem, considering the point of view of everyone involved;

- Discuss the possible effects of solutions;

- Find solutions that make everyone feel as good about themselves as possible;

- Implement agreements with sincere effort to make them work;
- Stay cool if agreements don't work at first;
- Give ourselves and each other permission to make mistakes with occasional feedback, but without shame-inducing criticism;
- Regularly reevaluate solutions to see how they're working;
- Criticize only behavior, never the person or personality;
- Make "I-statements," not "you-statements" about how we feel. Example: "I'm disappointed to hear this," not: "You make me furious;"
- Listen to each other *respectfully*, especially when we disagree;
- Never insult, call names, or make sarcastic remarks;
- Stick to the topic;
- Stay in the present and future – don't dredge up the past;
- Hold dialogues, not lectures;
- Try to answer each other, not withdraw or say, "I don't know," or “Do whatever you want;”
- Think realistically
  - don't think the worst right away, consider evidence
  - avoid "all or nothing" or "black and white," "never," and "always" thinking.

Signatures: ____

____

____

____

____

Everyone in the family should sign the agreement. Even two year-olds can make a crayon mark.

Solution-Finding Guide

Chores

Parents should come to the first regular weekly meeting with a list of all necessary chores. *Everyone* chooses equally from the chore list, allowing for differences in available time and special talents. (The two year-old can't change the oil or balance the checkbook; parents of teenagers can't wash the dishes if they have to go out to another job.) Family members must **negotiate** disagreements about choices.

With each item, the chooser must also indicate a sanction for failing to accomplish the chore.

In subsequent meetings, behavior problems that anyone in the family has should be aired.

Behavior problems (including problems that children might have with parents' behavior)

- Brain-storm solutions
  - Come up with as many as possible
  - Don't evaluate them during the brainstorming session and certainly don't dismiss them
  - Be creative, don't be afraid to suggest outlandish ideas, they sometimes work

- Decide the solution that is best for everybody, remembering that everybody's feelings are important

- Plan to implement the selected solution
  - Decide who will do what when where and how
  - Plan the consequence for compliance or non-compliance
  - Plan a time for evaluation of the implemented solution

- Implement the solution

- Evaluate the solution at the planned time.

Do's and Don'ts of Empowered Parenting

Parental Duties

- Provide unconditional love, compassion, and acceptance
- ***Model*** (children learn from *watching* you) the Five R's of parenting:
  - Resourcefulness
  - Responsibility
  - Respect
  - Relationship investment
  - Regulation of impulses and emotions
- Instill optimism
- Teach skills in negotiation/cooperation.

MODEL Solution finding

- *Do* stay focused on solutions
  Don't blame

- *Do* ask questions that elicit solutions from the child
  Don't solve the problem or offer unsolicited advice

- *Do* encourage the child to consider alternative solutions
  Don't imply that there is only one right way to solve problems

- *Do* encourage brainstorming of possible solutions
  Don't dismiss the child's ideas out of hand

MODEL Responsibility

- *Do* keep your commitments
  Don't break promises

- *Do* consider the feelings of others
  Don't act like the "Lord and Master"

- *Do* pick up after yourself
  Don't make others wait on you

- *Do* hold morals above convenience
  Don't justify your incorrect behavior

- *Do* be authoritative
  Don't be authoritarian

- *Do* admit to being unsure
  Don't pretend to know it all

- *Do* be truthful and honest
  Don't be phony, lie, or cheat

- *Do* show that power includes responsibility
  Don't exert power arbitrarily

MODEL Respect

- *Do* treat everyone with respect
  Don't ridicule anyone

- *Do* let the child speak for himself
  Don't speak for the child

- *Do* listen
  Don't interrupt

- *Do* reflect
  Don't react

- *Do* focus on uniqueness of each child
  Don't compare the child to other children, including siblings

- *Do* talk
  Don't yell, scream, or lecture

- *Do* let the child have his own childhood
  Don't use your childhood as a standard

- *Do* validate the child's feelings (affirm the child's right to have them)
  Don't invalidate the child's feelings (tell him what he really feels or what she doesn't have the right to feel)

MODEL Regulation of impulses, emotions

- *Do* ask the child to list the consequences of acting on impulse
  Don't lecture or moralize about consequences

- *Do* show compassion for self and others
  Don't blame or put down self and others

- *Do* take the child's perspective and compare it with your own
  Don't get locked in your own perspective

- *Do* express deeper feelings
  Don't express symptoms/defenses, e.g., shaming anger, anxiety, obsessions

- *Do* be flexible
  Don't be rigid

Guidance/Discipline

- *Do* empower (help the child find the solution)
  Don't engage in power struggles

- *Do* praise specific effort or accomplishment
  Don't praise the child

- *Do* express problems accurately
  Don't exaggerate or minimize

- *Do* teach the child how to *do* better
  Don't shame or humiliate the child

- *Do* set limits
  Don't hit or spank

- *Do* criticize specific behavior at specific times
  Don't criticize or label the child (lazy, dumb, liar, etc.)

- *Do* discipline specific behavior
  Don't discipline a "bad boy/girl"

- *Do* respectfully ask how the child can prevent the mistake in the future
  Don't threaten or punish

- *Do* withhold rewards or privileges
  Don't withdraw affection or threaten abandonment

- *Do* let the child learn
  Don't intervene too soon

- *Do* enhance the child's strengths
  Don't focus on the child's weaknesses

- *Do* respectfully confront
  Don't avoid

- *Do* attend to positive behavior
  Don't reinforce negative behavior with attention

- *Do* allow your child to make choices within parameters acceptable to you
  Don't sweat the small stuff or try to control everything

Instill Optimism

- *Do* enjoy the child
  Don't imply that the child is a burden

- *Do* learn from the child
  Don't assume you know it all

- *Do* play
  Don't tease (at the child's expense)

- *Do* teach the inherent Core Value of self and others
  Don't imply that the child is inferior or superior to others

- *Do* teach that mistakes are temporary, due to situation or particular effort, and usually correctable
  Don't imply that mistakes are permanent, irrevocable, or due to personality or lack of skills and talent

- *Do* teach that some tasks are negotiable and that cooperation is fun and productive
  Don't imply that all tasks and instructions are carved in stone and that cooperation is work, punishment, submission, or weakness

- *Do* kiss goodnight
  Don't send a child to bed in anger

- *Do* laugh with the child
  Don't take everything seriously

- *Do* sit with the child at meals
  Don't ignore the child while eating

- *Do* take walks together
  Don't always say, "go out and play"

- *Do* show pleasure to see the child after school
  Don't ignore child's homecoming or immediately discipline or make assignments

- *Do* hug the child a minimum of six times per day
  Don't be afraid to touch or "spoil" the child

- *Do* smile at the child frequently
  Don't scowl or frown

- *Do* make eye contact
  Don't glare

- *Do* be friendly and warm
  Don't seem aloof, closed, or distant

- *Do* speak softly
  Don't sound loud, hostile, or sarcastic

- *Do* relax
  Don't be tense, compulsive, or a perfectionist

SESSION 8: *Disagreement in the Compassionate Mode*

The primary goal in resolving disputes is that each person feels important, regarded, respected, and valuable and that no one feels put upon, taken advantage of, exploited, or used.

Step One: Define the problem *with explanation* (not *justification*) of why it's a problem, and ask for solutions.

> "Here's the problem, and this is why it's a problem for me. What do you think is the best solution?"
>
> Example: "I have a problem with the stereo being so loud, because I'm trying to concentrate on my work (or relax or watch TV, etc.). How can we work out this problem?"

If you disagree with the solution, don't *attack* or *put down* the other person.

- Validate the suggestion as a *possible* solution.
- State your reasons for disagreeing.
- Solicit another solution.

Example of a solution with which you'll disagree: "You could concentrate on your work later." Response: "Okay, that's one solution, but I need (want) to concentrate *now*. What's another solution?"

Step Two: Reach a *mutual* agreement about which solution to implement.

Step Three: Implement Solution, *with a commitment to make it work* (don't set it up to fail).

Step Four: Evaluate Solution after it's had a chance to work.

> "Our solution has been great; we don't have that problem anymore."
> "We need to review our solution to the trash problem; it's building up again in the kitchen."

Make a sincere attempt to understand your loved one's personal goals and preferences.

Example: People rarely share the same tolerance for mess (or compulsion for neatness). This often results in a no-win power struggle with everybody feeling put upon and resentful. A sincere attempt to understand both points of view is necessary:

> "I know it's a problem to carry your glass into the kitchen, because you like to feel like you can relax in your own home. And I appreciate when you do carry in your glass. I'm not trying to put a power trip on you, but it's important to me that the house looks neat. What do you think is a fair solution?"

"I don't mind carrying in my glass, if you wouldn't hassle me about it if I forget."

"If you make a sincere effort to remember to carry in your glass, I'll make a sincere effort not to hassle you if you really do forget. Is that fair?"

Adult Empowerment

A couple disagrees about when to have a second child. (Their baby is 10 months old.) Both need to make a *sincere* effort to understand the importance of the other's beliefs, goals, and desires, *and* to sympathize with any disappointment if the desire cannot be met. If they do not, their disagreement will get stuck in a destructive mode.

Disagreement in Destructive Mode

SHE	HE
I want to have a child now.	I want to wait till we can afford a child.
You're so selfish! It's always just what *you* want. All you think about is money! You're a cold, inconsiderate person!	You're so irresponsible! You're just like your mother! You never listen to reason! You're stupid, self-centered, and emotional!

Disagreement in the Compassionate Mode

Do not attempt if there is still any threat of abuse.	HE	SHE
1. Do HEALS™	**HEALS™**	**HEALS™**
2. State and validate the *other's* perspective	I know it's important for you to have a child now, because you're a caring and nurturing person.	I appreciate that it's important for you to be able to provide for our child and not to have our standard of living decline.
3. Disagree	I worry about not being able to meet expenses. I don't feel I make enough money to support a family the way I want to.	I feel that, if we wait, it will be that much harder for me to find work when the child's in school and I'm that much older.
4. Express your deepest emotions	I guess I'm insecure about earning a comfortable living.	I guess I feel insecure about finding a job when I'm older.
5. Validate the other's deepest emotions	I'll love you even if you can't find a job when you're older.	I'll love you no matter how much money you make.
6. Try reconciliation (If no agreement, start the process over.)	We don't have to wait; it's important to you to have a child now.	I don't mind waiting to have a child, because it's important to you.

Note: This couple knew what to write in the second box because they are merely citing the qualities they once loved about one another. He fell in love with her sensitivity, emotionality, and nurturing personality. She felt protected by his long-range financial planning and attention to detail. She got him more in touch with his own emotions, and he grounded her with a sense of financial reality. They were ideal complements to one another. This dispute, like so many power struggles, was entirely predictable from their early courtship. Power struggles very often result from the sense of betrayal we feel when loved ones criticize the things they used to love about us.

Use the grid below to resolve disagreements compassionately.

Do not attempt if there is still any threat of abuse.	**YOU**	**HER**
1. Do HEALS™	**HEALS™**	**HEALS™**
2. State and validate the *other's* perspective		
3. Disagree		
4. Express your deepest emotions		
5. Validate the other's deepest emotions		
6. Try reconciliation (If no agreement, start the process over.)		

Empowerment Formula

1. Validate

2. Respectfully disagree

The order is crucial. If you disagree before you validate, you will not be heard.

Time Dimensions for Recovering From Abuse

THE PAST	THE PRESENT	THE FUTURE
blame	**responsibility**	**responsibility**
danger	**safety**	**safety**
insulting	respect	trust
injured feelings	value	intimacy
emotional battering	support	support
physical harm	mutual growth	mutual growth
police, court, jail		

There are three time dimensions to recovery from abuse, each characterized by its own set of behaviors and challenges. Know which reactions are from the past and **label** them as leftovers of the past. *Blaming* and threats to safety will certainly bring back the past. They must give way to responsibility, respect, value, support, and mutual growth. Only when the behaviors listed under the **present** are firmly established can you expect to move into the future with reinstated intimacy and trust.

Once betrayed, the road to restored trust is long and slow. Trying to renew trust too soon sets up both parties for almost certain failure. No matter how much you might want to trust someone who has hurt you, your brain will not let you drop defenses completely, which is the necessary step toward true intimacy.

The slow recovery from betrayed trust is due to the survival implications of pain. The brain processes pain on a separate neural network that ensures priority attention. This creates an overly sensitive, involuntary, almost reflexive response to avoid the recurrence of pain.

For example, the recently burned hand flinches near a stove. The *heat* of the stove stimulates an alarm of pain. This automatic "flinch" persists until new experience shows that pain is unlikely to recur, as long as behavior around the heat is careful.

Unfortunately, the pain alarm in attachment relationships often links directly with interest, compassion, trust, affection, and intimacy. The involuntary "flinch" will likely come at the reinstatement of any of these. An alarm in the brain will sound at the most inopportune time, such as a warm moment or an embrace. This involuntary reaction causes guilt in the person experiencing it and shame in the partner. Both will likely appear as anger or resentment, causing further damage to the attachment bond.

Post Traumatic Stress

Abuse of any kind often produces symptoms of post traumatic stress. These include:

- Flashbacks of past abuse (sometimes from past relationships or childhood)
- Anxiety or anger that comes out of nowhere
- Confusion
- Impaired decision making

- Depression
- Aggressive impulses.

These symptoms have no meaning about personality. They are natural stages of healing for many people. They are merely a delayed physiological response to past abuse that mean nothing about you as a person.

Healing *always* occurs in discreet stages. Take a cut on the hand as an example. The wound must pass through several distinct stages of healing. The first is an elevation of heart rate to bleed out any bacteria that might have entered the wound. The second stage is a precipitous drop in heart rate to decrease the amount of lost blood. (The steep drop in blood pressure is why some people faint.) The third stage is massive migration of white blood cells to the area of the insult. Dead white cells make pus. Blood congeals and forms a soft scab, then a hard one, followed by complete healing. All the while, the body remains hypersensitive to further injury of the wounded area – if someone bumps into the wounded area, your instinct is to deck him.

What happens if you interfere with any of these stages of healing? You're back to square one, of course.

Unfortunately, the psychological effects of abuse take longer to heal than a cut on the hand. Only an uninterrupted flow of compassion will renew a bond capable of enduring over the long run. Any interference with the discreet stages of healing, like saying, "Get over it," or, "Let it go already," is the emotional equivalent of picking at the scab. It will not only retard the healing process but run the risk of returning it to square one.

Both parties must understand that the seeming rejection implied by diminished trust and intimacy is actually rejection of the **past**, abusive relationship, and not of the **present**, healing relationship. This knowledge will limit flashbacks and shorten the time required for replenishment of trust, love, and uninhibited intimacy.

Fortunately, trust is never an all-or-nothing choice. The immediate goal of all parties of a relationship that has suffered betrayal cannot be 100% trust. The immediate goal must be 10% trust. Then 20%. Then 30%, 40%, and so on. In attachment relationships, we owe unconditional compassion. But trust, especially once betrayed, must be earned.

Earning back trust requires that the **impulse to punish** be regulated. The impulse to punish is a signal of unhealed hurt. Your entire emotional energy should go into healing the hurt rather than avenging it.

Session 9: *The Great Threat of Intimacy*

Two great fears reside deep in the core self of most human beings. The first is **fear of engulfment**: If she (or he) gets too close, the self will be:

Exposed and vulnerable
Overwhelmed
Disintegrated or
Absorbed by another self.

The second great fear in the heart of most humans is **fear of abandonment:** If she/he moves too far away, the self will:

Lose identity
Lose value
Disintegrate.

Although every human being has these two great fears, childhood and adult attachment experience exaggerate them.

For example, **rejected** or **neglected** children are likely to have an exaggerated fear of abandonment, while **abused** or **dominated** children or those **not loved for who they really are**, may have exaggerated fear of engulfment – if loved ones get too close they will hurt and overwhelm the self.

How to tell fear of abandonment from genuinely missing someone: Fear of abandonment powers your relationship if you feel anxious and terribly lonely when not with that person, but when you *are* together, it really isn't all that great. In other words, once abandonment anxiety subsides, there seems to be little genuine bond.

How to tell fear of engulfment from the mere desire for a little privacy: Fear of engulfment dominates your relationship if you can't wait to get away from that person. But as soon as she's gone you start missing her. In contrast, the need for privacy and distance tends to ebb and flow more gradually.

The Desperate Dance of Pursuer-Distancer

There are two common ways of coping with fear of abandonment and fear of engulfment:

- Smothering the fear with closeness – the **pursuer**
- Avoiding the fear by keeping others at a distance – the **distancer.**

The **pursuer** continually wants more closeness and intimacy than the other can tolerate. The **pursuer** sets up all sorts of manipulations for closeness and intimacy, while the **distancer** confounds and distracts from these, using other people, work, alcohol or drugs, TV, hobbies, etc., as distancing tactics.

Neither the pursuer nor the distancer self-regulates fear of abandonment and fear of engulfment; each relies on the other to set limits. So pursuers never have to worry about how much closeness they really want; they rely on distancers to decide how much they will get. Distancers never have to decide how much closeness *they* want, as long as they occasionally relent in their rejection "for the sake of the pursuer."

The Unavoidable Pain of Pursuing and Distancing

- The pursuer-distancer dance always ends in **rejection**.

- The accumulated shame – of rejecting a loved one and of being rejected by a loved one – takes on a life of its own, stimulating anger and resentment and causing enormous damage to the attachment bond.

Pursuers stop pursuing when the weight of continual rejection becomes too much to bear. When they finally back off, their partners often start their own pursuit in a dramatic role reversal.

Though most typical of relationships between lovers, the pursuer-distancer dance can afflict *any* attachment relationship. A common example is the adult child rigorously pursuing the love, acceptance, or approval of a rejecting or aloof or preoccupied parent. This tends to be a same-sex phenomenon (though certainly not always), with adult sons pursuing distant fathers and adult daughters pursuing withholding or critical mothers.

Guilt over childhood neglect or abuse often drives parents to pursue adult children. Those whose parental years featured alcoholism, overwork, favoritism of other children, depression, affairs, etc., are especially susceptible to this sort of pursuit.

Needy parents often find their young children and adolescents distancing to maintain sufficient space for the development of their own personalities, values, opinions, and interests.

Young children and adolescents pursue distancing parents to the best of their limited abilities, working hard through school performance, cuteness, athletics, or any other means to earn their parents' love.

The only way out of the painful and frustrating dance of the pursuer-distancer is for each person to self-regulate fear of abandonment and fear of engulfment.

Fear of abandonment and engulfment grow worse when we expect loved ones to regulate them. When not self-regulated, fear of abandonment keeps us in bad relationships (and prevents them from becoming better), while fear of engulfment keeps us out of good relationships.

Fear of abandonment is fear of feeling incomplete without the other.

Regulation:

1. Do **HEALS™**. (If this person fails to love me, it does not mean that I'm unimportant, not valuable, unacceptable, or unlovable.)

2. Realize that you can be disappointed, sad, and lonely, but the self is not at stake, there is no loss of Core Value or self-esteem, if this person fails to love you.

Fear of engulfment is fear of feeling overwhelmed by the other. This is harder to regulate, because it usually includes hidden fear of abandonment. (If people get too close they will see the real me that is unlovable and that cannot love.)

Regulation:

1. Steps 1 and 2 above, to regulate fear of abandonment, because it is usually hidden under fear of engulfment.

2. *Acceptance that*:
   - *Everyone* has a part of the self that is not lovable and that cannot love and that we must emphasize the more important loving and lovable part.

   - You can regulate *any* internal experience.

   - **The self is too solid and well integrated to be overwhelmed or absorbed by another.**

Closeness Regulation

After the initial, romantic phase of the relationship, men and women seldom agree on how close or how far apart they want to be. Research shows that in successful long-term relationships the degree of closeness ebbs and flows. Sometimes the partners feel close and sometimes they do not. Most successful couples have developed ways to negotiate about closeness. The following are some tips to help with regulating closeness in your relationship.

First of all, in everyone, the degree of desired closeness:

1. Varies greatly from week to week, day to day, even moment to moment

2. Depends on levels of stress (though some people want more closeness under stress while others want more distance)

3. Is governed by two great fears (both intensified by childhood rejection, neglect, abuse): **fear of abandonment** and **fear of engulfment**

Dysfunctional Distance Regulation:

1. Uses anger as a distance regulator
2. Interprets distance regulation as rejection.

Functional (growth oriented) Closeness Regulation:

1. Recognizes and respects one another's varying needs and desires for closeness and distance (It's okay to want closeness and it's okay to want distance.)

2. Communicates directly and compassionately about closeness-regulation.

More Conflict Resolution Skills

The Cardinal Rules:

1. **Each party must self-regulate anger to allow negotiation on the issue.**

2. **The ultimate goal of solution-seeking must be that everyone feels important, regarded, valued, and respected. Anything less makes the problem worse.**

3. **Recognize your competence, growth, creativity, and compassion. Empower your loved ones by supporting their competence, growth, creativity, and compassion.**

Although the cardinal rules alone will help you solve most problems, here are a few additional rules to help settle disputes. But conflict resolution skills can only correct deficits in communication. You have to *want* to communicate, and you have to *care* about what your loved ones feel for any attempts at conflict resolution to work.

- *Narrow* the dispute as much as possible, focusing on specific behaviors at specific times. Don't bring in past hurts or offenses. Don't say, "You always," or "You never."

- Talk only about behavior, never the "personality" of loved ones. Example: "I felt uncomfortable when you said that," not, "You bitch!" or "You're a cold, inconsiderate person!" Example: "I have a different perception," not, "You're a liar," or "You're crazy," or "You make up things in your head."

- Make "I" statements. "I feel upset when you say that," rather than, "You make me angry." In the first case you own the feeling and have power over it; in the second, you blame the feeling on your partner and render yourself powerless.

- Create new options to negotiate whenever possible. Example: "I can't get home in time to go to dinner, but we'll have time to see a movie."

- If new options are not possible, negotiate, with ***mutual respect*** and ***sincerity***, until you can decide to whom the issue is more important. For instance, it's important for her to go out that night and relax after a tense day, and it's important for him to go home and relax after an exhausting day. "I know you've had a tense day, and if I weren't so beat, I'd go out with you to help you unwind. But I'm just too tired." Note: The way to communicate importance is with passion or conviction and with honesty and sincerity *not* with anger.

Remember, the key to conflict resolution is self-regulation, self-empowerment, and empowerment of your partner or child or parent, along with the *sincere* desire to have everyone feel as good as possible about the resolution.

SESSION 10: *Resentment*

What happens when a family member gives in or goes along just to keep the peace or avoid a hassle, or because he/she is too tired to argue?

a. **Everyone feels okay about themselves**

b. **The creation of resentment and hostility that can last indefinitely.**

When resentment is high, sex is bad or nonexistent. Resentment is a defensive form of low-grade anger. As such it destroys intimacy. Its defensive nature keeps us from letting down barriers and resuming the vulnerability necessary for true intimacy. Though all forms of intimacy suffer with resentment, sexuality may be the most noticeable.

Resentment may be the most complex of all human emotions. The result of *every* **power struggle**, it's extremely difficult to resolve, due to its many components. It may account for most of the ill-feeling we experience, because it never really ends. Its continuous nature consumes so much emotional energy that it eventually blocks out most interest and enjoyment. When resentment takes a foothold in your life, it becomes a joyless drive to get things done. You'll do everything you have to do, but you won't be interested in much and you'll enjoy less. Because it feels so bad, resentment often drives people to drink and use drugs for relief.

Components of resentment:

1. **Regret**
2. **Remorse**
3. **Shame**
4. **Self-anger**
5. **Anger** at opponent in the power struggle
6. **Anger at others** in general.

Example: I agreed to have my brother-in-law, whom I don't like, move in with us, because my wife wanted it. I keep noticing things about his behavior that irritate me. I take it out on my wife – if it wasn't for her, I wouldn't have to put up with him.

1. I **regret** my brother-in-law moving in.

2. I'm **sorry** that I misled my wife into thinking I could stand it.

3. I feel **shame** that I can't do this for her, so I continually look for justification of my failure – her brother snores, has a poor sense of humor, doesn't comb his hair right, etc.

4. I'm **angry at her** for not appreciating how much of a bother this would be and for not understanding me. I'm angry at her for not wanting what I want, for not feeling the way I do about this, and for not agreeing with me.

5. I'm **angry at myself** for failing to realize how much bother it would be and for not being assertive about how I really felt.

6. Because resentment puts me in a bad mood, I get **angry at other people** about little things, like traffic, the news, my team losing, the baby crying, the phone ringing, etc.

Preventing Resentment

1. Resolve disputes and make decisions with closure. Be sure that you can say:
   "I'm convinced that this is the best thing I can do (at this time), and I *commit* myself to making it work."

2. Feel good about the resolution. This means *expressing shame*:
   "I know it sounds childish, but I'm afraid that if your brother moves in, I won't get enough of your time, and I care about having time with you."

NOTE: If you don't express shame, it will undermine all attempts to make the solution work, as well as any attempt at true intimacy.

3. Reward yourself with a feeling of well being for doing the right thing, whatever that turns out to be.

4. Accept responsibility for your decision.
   With responsibility, you regulate your own experience.
   With resentment, your feelings are in the power of someone else.

5. If it turns out that you made a mistake, make the most of it:
   "I made a mistake in *my* decision, but what can I do to repair, grow, and learn from the mistake?"

Other Kinds of Resentment, Caused by:

- Not getting to participate in a decision
- We're told, "You do this."
- The opinions and expectations of others
- Not getting expected or desired:
  - help
  - appreciation
  - consideration
  - praise or reward
  - affection

Steps in regulating these kinds of resentment:

1. Say explicitly what you desire and expect.
2. Internalize your own appreciation and reward.
3. Recognize the rights of everyone in the family.

The Chain of Resentment

The continuous nature of resentment creates a self-linking chain that grows completely on its own. Past resentments seem to attract present offenses, forming an ever longer and heavier chain.

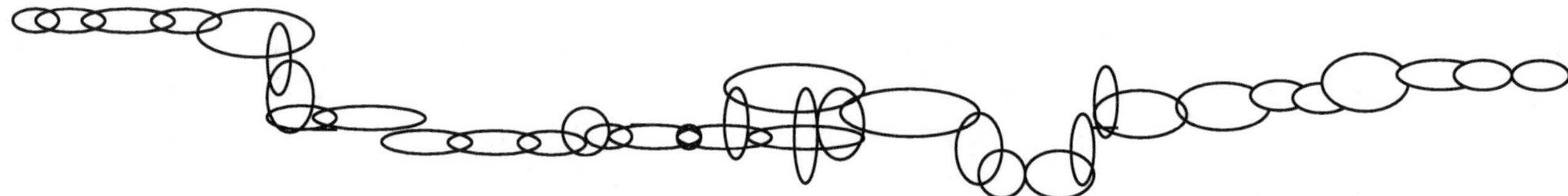

For example, a link is added to the chain of resentment when I resent my wife for going to bed without kissing me goodnight. That event gets linked onto the night before, when she tried to kiss me against my will. Naturally I didn't want her to kiss me, after she wouldn't help me with the dishes. This links onto the night before that, when she did the dishes behind my back, implying that I wasn't able to do a simple household chore. You get the idea. Once the most important things in life are bound by chains of hidden resentment, you can resent someone for doing something *and* for not doing it.

The Chain of Resentment in relationships is never just about the relationship. It includes incidents from work and from past relationships, extending back to childhood. Resentment makes you blame the closest person for your *generalized* negative mood and ill-feeling.

In its more advanced stages, resentment extends into the future. That's when your expectation of someone disappointing you becomes self-fulfilling prophecy. I fully expect her to do something (or not do something) to provoke still more resentment. If she's nice, she has something up her sleeve. I'll need to watch her more closely. "The weekend's going okay so far, but she'll find some way to screw it up."

The tremendous effort required to drag the Chain of Resentment through life makes us hyper-vigilant for possible offenses, lest they "sneak up" on us. This creates frequent sour moods and an atmosphere wherein no offense is too trivial or too unrealistic to be added as yet another link to the chain of resentment. In other words, like bacteria in a laboratory culture, **resentment breeds resentment**. So we will find reasons for resentment in the daily newspaper, in traffic patterns, in a dearth of parking places, in the temperature of drinking water, in other people's tastes, thoughts, opinions, feelings, and so on.

A few points about the architecture of a chain are worth noting. First of all, if you pick up a chain by one link, are you holding just that link or the weight of the whole chain? Resentment is never about a discreet incident or just one link. The Chain of Resentment does not distinguish important matters from petty or trivial ones – they're all links on the chain and therefore carry the weight of the whole chain. That's why nothing is too petty to resent.

Resentment and Violence

Virtually all initiated violence (not in self-defense or defense of loved ones) follows a long chain of resentment. For example, suppose you are at baseline arousal, with no resentment or anger of any kind. An obnoxious event, like someone shouting something about your mother as he speeds by, is likely to get you about 30% aroused, which will get no worse that sarcasm – you'll want to shout something about his mother in return. That kind of anger dissipates in a few minutes. In a couple of hours you won't even remember that it happened.

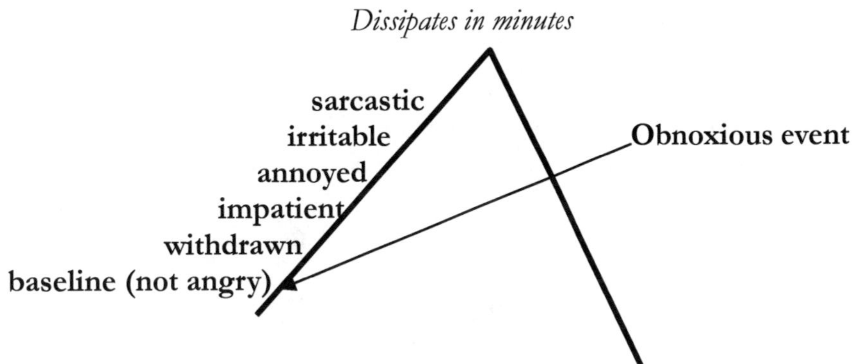

But if you are resentful about something that happened or might happen at home or work or on the road, you're already about 20-30% aroused – *more*, if it's a link on a long and heavy chain of resentment. That same obnoxious event will get you about 60-70% aroused. There you begin to get aggressive, with a hair-trigger mechanism for escalation, should there be any negative response to your aggression. This kind of anger can stay with you for days as you keep rehashing it in your mind.

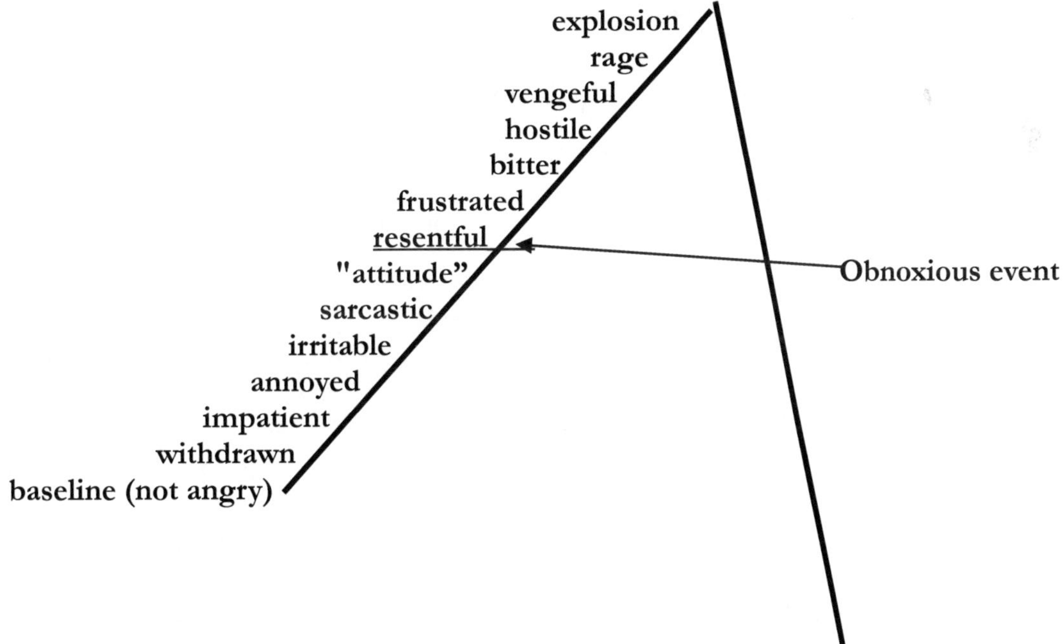

Add caffeine, nicotine, anxiety, or a startle response to the mix, and the adrenaline rush of anger on top of resentment can easily go through the roof.

Resentment and Health

Most of the ill-health effects of anger reviewed in Session Two result from chronic resentment. In terms of the health risks that prolonged resentment creates, you take time off your life for every minute that you spend in resentment.

Bearing the Chain

Here's an exercise to help you appreciate how resentment affects you. Make a list of all the things about your attachment relationships that make you resentful. (If you are honest and thorough, your list will contain many petty and trivial matters, as well as a few serious ones.) From a hardware store, buy the kind of chain that allows you to add or subtract links with a simple snapping motion. (If you can't find such a chain, buy a bunch of heavy nails.) For each item on your resentment list, add a link to the chain (or drop in five nails). Put the chain (or nails) in a sturdy bag. **Carry the bag around with you constantly.** This means taking it everywhere, to work, to the store, to the bathroom, to get the mail – *everywhere*! This is precisely what we do with resentment.

When you can stand the weight of the bag no longer, you are ready to resolve resentment.

Breaking the Chain

The first thing to realize about the terrible Chain of Resentment is that you don't *have* to feel it. The experience of resentment is a *choice* you make.

The second thing to realize is that the Chain of Resentment binds the *self* more than anyone else. Breaking the chain of resentment means unburdening the *self*, *setting the self free.*

Can't Let Go

No one can just "let go" of resentment. You can resolve resentment only by investing more value in your life. The more you value, the less you will resent. The more compassionate you are, the less you are able to resent.

Forgiveness

The emotional opposite of resentment is forgiveness. However, forgiveness *does not mean condoning* or *overlooking* the offense. It does not mean *reconciling* with someone who has hurt you. Neither does it require that you forego legal procedures of justice.

Forgiveness means letting go of the **compulsion to punish**, in the realization that we cannot harm others, particularly those we love or have loved, without harming the self.

Just as we cannot sustain compassion for others without self-compassion, we cannot forgive others without **self-forgiveness**. The power of forgiveness, like all genuine power, originates **within**.

Take Back Your Power: *Self-Forgiveness*

Identify the *deepest* core hurt stimulated by each item on your resentment list. (The one you made as part of your homework assignment.) By forgiving yourself for allowing your Core Value to be lowered, you take back power over your emotional well being.

Item 1. I forgive myself for losing sight of my Core Value and feeling (name core hurt): ____________________________, when he/she____________________________.

Item 2. I forgive myself for losing sight of my Core Value and feeling (name core hurt): ____________________________, when he/she____________________________.

Item 3. I forgive myself for losing sight of my Core Value and feeling (name core hurt): ____________________________, when he/she____________________________.

Item 4. I forgive myself for losing sight of my Core Value and feeling (name core hurt): ____________________________, when he/she____________________________.

Item 5. I forgive myself for losing sight of my Core Value and feeling (name core hurt): ____________________________, when he/she ____________________________.

Item 6. I forgive myself for losing sight of my Core Value and feeling (name core hurt): ____________________________, when he/she____________________________.

Item 7. I forgive myself for losing sight of my Core Value and feeling (name core hurt): ____________________________, when he/she____________________________.

Item 8. I forgive myself for losing sight of my Core Value and feeling (name core hurt): ____________________________, when he/she____________________________.

Item 9. I forgive myself for losing sight of my Core Value and feeling (name core hurt): ____________________________, when he/she____________________________.

Item 10. I forgive myself for losing sight of my Core Value and feeling (name core hurt): ____________________________, when he/she____________________________.

The Road to Genuine Power: *Forgiveness of Others*

1. **Forgiveness does not mean condoning bad behavior**

2. **Forgiveness means forgoing the impulse to punish, in recognition of the harm it does to the self.**

Item 1. I forgive you for reminding me that I sometimes feel (name core hurt): _________________.

Item 2. I forgive you for reminding me that I sometimes feel (name core hurt): _________________.

Item 3. I forgive you for reminding me that I sometimes feel (name core hurt): _________________.

Item 4. I forgive you for reminding me that I sometimes feel (name core hurt): _________________.

Item 5. I forgive you for reminding me that I sometimes feel (name core hurt): _________________.

Item 6. I forgive you for reminding me that I sometimes feel (name core hurt): _________________.

Item 7. I forgive you for reminding me that I sometimes feel (name core hurt): _________________.

Item 8. I forgive you for reminding me that I sometimes feel (name core hurt): _________________.

Item 9. I forgive you for reminding me that I sometimes feel (name core hurt): _________________.

Item 10. I forgive you for reminding me that I sometimes feel (name core hurt): _________________.

The Requirements of Intimacy

Once you completely remove the barrier of resentment, it is possible to fully renew intimacy. However, the only standard for how much intimacy makes a satisfying relationship is that both partners agree.

Intimacy requires:

1. **Caring** about what a person is, caring about what he or she **thinks** and **feels**, not what you think he or she should think and feel. This means caring when he or she feels bad about something. It means **respecting your differences**.

2. **Self disclosure:** Freely revealing anything about yourself, including some things you might be ashamed of. This kind of emotional exposure heals the self and draws partners closer together.

3. **Protecting the attachment bond:** trying, especially in disputes, *not* to threaten abandonment or engulfment (hurting, dominating). Note: if there is abuse, there has to be a threat of abandonment to protect everyone involved.

Intimacy Test:

- Do you want to accept that your partner has thoughts, beliefs, preferences, and feelings that *differ* from yours? Can you respect those differences? Can you cherish your partner despite them? Can you accept them without trying to change them?

- Can you disclose *anything* about yourself, including your deepest thoughts and feelings, without fear of rejection, criticism, or misunderstanding?

- Is the message of your relationship, "grow, expand, create, disclose, reveal?" Or is it, "hide, conceal, think only in certain ways, behave only in certain ways, feel only certain things?"

- Does this relationship offer both parties optimal growth? Can you both develop into the greatest persons you can be?

Red Flag of potential abuse: *blamers.* People who blame their emotional states or behavior on someone or something else in dating will eventually turn the blame to you.

SESSION 11: *Consolidate Gains*

Research shows that people better internalize information they have learned if they can summarize it in front of other people.

In this session, each group member stands and states at least three things gained from the class.

SESSION 12: Relapse Prevention

Moving toward the Future

Monthly Checklists for Preventing Relapse

Bite of the Vampire

The emotional pain of attachment abuse works like the **bite of the vampire.** Once we get the fangs, we *always* have them and will always be visited by a recurring impulse to make others like ourselves. **Relapse** is forgetting that we have the fangs or forgetting that we can and must keep them retracted.

Early Warning Signs That the Fangs are Inching Forward

- Resentment
- Jealousy/Envy
- Getting angry in traffic
- Irritability
- Restlessness
- Impatience
- Moodiness
- Trouble sleeping (sleep too little or too much)
- Isolation (don't want to go out or see friends)
- Don't want your family to go out or socialize
- Emotional chill, closed off from loved ones
- Persistent sadness, loneliness
- An *urge* to control or spy on family members
    - discouraging them from friendships
    - wanting them to tell you their every move
    - listening to their phone calls
    - reading their email or snail mail.

Monthly Checklist

The following is an utterly honest attempt to monitor my behavior and attitudes toward loved ones. (Put a check for each thing you have done during the month.)

Self-Compassion

1. Validated my core hurts and accessed my Core Value on a regular basis	
2. Recognized the Core Value of others on a regular basis	

Compassion for Loved Ones

3. Validated their core hurts	
4. Empowered them to seek solutions from their Core Value	

Communication Skills

5. Accurately reflected loved one's meaning	

6. Maintained attitude of respect	
7. Tried to find some truth in what loved ones said, even when I disagreed with most of it	
8. Responded to underlying positive wishes beneath complaints (For instance, a complaint about you not calling has the underlying positive wish to feel more connected.)	
9. Expressed my *true* feelings, not symptoms and defenses, i.e., core hurts, not anger or resentment they cause	

Communication Blocks

10. Moralized, preached, or lectured	
11. Ordered, directed, demanded	
12. Advised, gave solutions	
13. Interpreted, analyzed	
14. Interrogated	

Fighting Dirty

15. Failed to use compassion	
16. Blamed, accused, showed disrespect	
17. Threatened abandonment	
18. Predicted bleak future (you'll fail, you won't make it, no one will love you)	
19. Withdrew, ignored (the "silent treatment")	
20. Distracted, diverted	
21. My unregulated anger created hostile atmosphere	
22. Denial of personal responsibility ("I'm the victim!")	
23. Wanted revenge	
24. Expressed martyrdom	
25. Manipulated (hidden agendas)	

Abuse

26. Tried to hurt the feelings of loved ones	
27. Called them names, insulted, or ridiculed them	
28. Criticized personality rather than behavior	

29. Attacked self-esteem	
30. Threatened them	
31. Tried to humiliate them (knock them down a peg)	

Strategies for Preventing Relapse

- Rehearse **HEALS**™ at the earliest sign of relapse.
- Communicate with your partner about the early warning signs.
- Call a friend or a group member or the group leader.
- Come back to the Core Value Workshop at any time for any session, at *no cost.* Once you pay for your 14 sessions, you have a *lifetime membership* (unless court ordered to return).
- Exercise (improves mood).
- Eat well:
  - Avoid substances that stimulate anxiety or depression, such as caffeine, nicotine, drugs and alcohol, excessive salt, sugar, and preservatives;
  - Take vitamin supplements, particularly B's and C.
- Do something nice for yourself.
- Do something nice for loved ones.

WARNING!!!

- Emotional regulation skills deteriorate during alcohol and drug use!
- Most relapse that happens in the first year following treatment occurs in the *first three months* after completion of the group. This high stress time requires extra vigilance to keep the fangs retracted.
- Subsequent offences will have different consequences that will not be as pleasant as this class.

Final homework assignment

A Statement of Compassion

This is an exercise in **pride.** It shows the difference between what you were in the past and what you have become in the present.

Formally writing out the **Statement of Compassion** is important, whether or not you actually send it.

Note: This is an exercise in healing, not in blame. Don't attempt to *justify* whatever hurt you did, for that will *keep open your wounds.* **Don't say,** "I only hurt you because you hurt me." Healing means you have learned that you ***don't have to*** **hurt back**, that **hurting back only hurts you more**.

Do *not* ask for forgiveness in your compassion statement. True compassion respects that forgiveness has to do entirely with the aggrieved person's own healing process. It may never come. But it is unnecessary to your healing and your compassionate identity.

You have the option of doing this assignment in the form of a letter. If you choose to do a letter, you must cover all six points that follow.

Statement of Compassion

1. State *how* you hurt your loved one. What did you do? List all instances of *verbal*, *emotional*, or *physical abuse.*

2. What effects has your behavior had on that person or persons, *especially* on his/her capacity to sustain the attachment emotions: *interest, compassion, trust, intensity of affection, intimacy,* and *commitment?*

3. What effects has your behavior had on you, *especially* on your capacity to sustain the attachment emotions: *interest, compassion, trust, intensity of affection, intimacy, commitment?*

4. Did your behavior make the situation better or worse?

5. State how you intend in the future to negotiate and cooperate rather than engage in power struggles (include the difference between negotiation/cooperation and power struggles).

6. State *specifically* what you need to do to keep the fangs retracted in the future so that you will never intentionally hurt a loved one.

SESSIONS 13-14

Each group member stands and reads his or her *Statement of Compassion* aloud. The rest of the time is spent processing how new skills and information have affected the lives of participants.

HOMEWORK ASSIGNMENTS DUE WEEKS 2-14

Always look at the top of the page to see in which session the assignment is due.

DUE SESSION 2 **Name**

Even mild motivation to control, stonewall (silent treatment), or emotionally abuse produces major physiological changes. **Your body reacts to this arousal long before you conscious mind knows that anything is wrong.** You must know what arousal feels like in different parts of your body.

Write what arousal feels like in each of the following. (Think hard to answer each question. ***Do not write, "nothing" or "N/A".*** That would mean you are dead. Such answers must include a note from the coroner.)

Head

Eyes

Mouth

Jaw

Neck

Shoulders

Chest

Stomach

Back

Hands

Please list your goals of ***self-improvement*** for this course.

1.

2.

3.

Please circle what *you* will need to do to accomplish your goals.

Think Learn Work hard Other:

How will you know that you are achieving your goals? What changes will you notice in yourself?

In how you feel?

In how you behave?

DUE SESSION 2 **Name**

SHADOWS OF THE HEART

1. What does a child feel when he or she witnesses emotional or physical abuse of a parent?

2. What kind of long-term effect does witnessing violence have on children?

3. What kind of effect does violence have on a man or woman victim?

4. Is he or she likely to be defensive or aggressive in reaction?

5. When you see angry or resentful people, how do you think they look?

6. How does *your* anger look to others?

7. How does your anger look to your spouse?

8. How does your anger look to your children?

DUE SESSION 3 **Name**

Core Value Bank

The *Core Value Bank* is designed as a repository of your core value, a kind of bank account of important things. You can think of each of the eight segments as a safety deposit box containing images or icons of some of the most important things to and about you. The Core Value Bank is itself an image of your *internal* value. The images it contains, while they might correspond to things in the world, reside *within* you. They are *always* there, ready to give you strength whenever you need it. Each time you see, hear, smell, touch, or taste something in the world similar to the contents of your Core Value Bank, it will remind you of your core value and thereby activate it. In other words, you will be motivated to improve, appreciate, connect, or protect. The next time you see a sunset, for example, it will not only seem beautiful, it will remind you of your core value.

The best thing about the Core Value Bank is that you make deposits at the same time you make withdrawals. You will *never* run out of core value.

After you fill in the boxes, we'll put your Bank to use as a tool of emotional reconditioning. Get ready for magic.

Your **basic humanity** safe deposit box is already filled in. This is the emotion you felt when you imagined helping and comforting the desperate child.

Meaning and purpose statements:

3. The *most* important thing about you as a person.
4. The *most* important thing about your life in general.

Love: Fill in the names of your loved ones. You're writing their names, but the emotional content of this box will be the actual love you feel for them.

Spiritual: Fill in a symbol (a drawing, mark, or word will do) of something that has spiritual importance to you. It can be religious, natural, cosmic, or social – anything will do, as long as it connects you to something larger than the self, which, while you are connected to it, seems more important than your everyday, mundane, or selfish concerns.

Nature: Name, draw, or describe a nature scene that makes you value, i.e., something that you feel is beautiful.

Creativity: Identify a piece of art, music, or other human creation that makes you feel value.

Community: Identify a sense of community connection, for example, a church, school, work, or neighborhood.

Compassion: List three compassionate things you have done. Don't think of Mother Theresa kind of compassion. These can be relatively small gestures, when you helped or comforted someone else, with no material gain to you.

My Core Value Bank

Basic Humanity	Meaning & Purpose	Love	Spiritual
The emotions I felt as I imagined rescuing and comforting the desperate child:	The most important thing about me as a person: The most important thing about my life in general:	The people I love:	My spiritual connection:
Nature	**Creativity**	**Community**	**Compassion**
Something beautiful in nature:	Something beautiful human made (art, music, architecture, furniture, etc.):	My community connection:	Compassionate things I have done: 1. 2. 3.

DUE SESSION 4 **Name**

Building Your Core Value Shield

In medieval times, knights engraved on their shields and protective armor symbols of the things that they believed protected them, made them strong, and helped them to do their best.

Your **Core Value Shield** will protect you from any abusive behavior by others and empower you to be as strong as possible to avoid any accidental or purposeful abuse of others.

For your Shield of Core Value, make a list of your strengths, assets, accomplishments, and your best qualities – the things that make you strong.

1.

2.

3.

4.

5.

6.

7.

8.

9.

10.

DUE SESSION 4 **Name**

Evidence of My Core Value
Things I have done to improve bad experiences: 1. 2. 3.
Things I appreciate: 1. 2. 3.
Things I do to emotionally connect with people I love: 1. 2. 3.
Things I do to protect my loved ones: 1. 2. 3.

DUE SESSION 4 **Name**

HEALS™ LOG

I have rehearsed **HEALS™** ______ times this week (minimum 72 times). **HEALS™ requires *practice* to make it automatic and to get its full healing benefit.**

Write out the steps of **HEALS™**:

H-
E-
A-
L-
S-

I hurt the feelings of my significant other or children this week _____ (YES/No).
If no, congratulate yourself! If yes, how many times? _______

I hurt the body of my significant other or children this week _____ (YES/No).
If no, congratulate yourself! If yes, describe what you did:

Power Log

This week I felt:

• Irritable	**A lot**	**Some**	**Hardly**	**None**
• Grouchy	**A lot**	**Some**	**Hardly**	**None**
• Annoyed	**A lot**	**Some**	**Hardly**	**None**
• Impatient	**A lot**	**Some**	**Hardly**	**None**
• Angry in traffic	**A lot**	**Some**	**Hardly**	**None**
• Like blaming someone	**A lot**	**Some**	**Hardly**	**None**
• Like making other people do things	**A lot**	**Some**	**Hardly**	**None**
• Like getting revenge	**A lot**	**Some**	**Hardly**	**None**
• Like hurting someone	**A lot**	**Some**	**Hardly**	**None**

What always **motivates** my anger, attitude, anxiety, irritability, grouchiness, impatience, restlessness, impulse to blame, hurt, or desire to get revenge?

Someone else's behavior **my core hurt** **the situation**

What can I do to make it *better*?

Get back at them
Do HEALS™
Hope it will pass

What always motivates other people's attitudes, anger, anxiety, irritability, grouchiness, impatience, and restlessness or impulse to blame, hurt, or get revenge?

Someone else's behavior | **their core hurts** | **the situation**

What can I do to make it better?

Get back at them
Do HEALS™
Hope it will pass

Self-Concept (write out)

"I believe in my Core Value. I want to act in my long term and short term best interests."

Self-Esteem (write out)

"I accept myself, even if my behavior needs to change."

This week I felt the power to:

• Regulate anger, anxiety, attitudes, resentment	**A lot**	**Some**	**Hardly**	**None**
• Choose behaviors in short *and* long term best interest	**A lot**	**Some**	**Hardly**	**None**
• Be flexible (true to myself while adapting to others)	**A lot**	**Some**	**Hardly**	**None**
• Feel self-compassion (go deeper to reconnect to Core Value)	**A lot**	**Some**	**Hardly**	**None**
• Feel compassion for others (go deeper to validate their Core Value)	**A lot**	**Some**	**Hardly**	**None**

When someone ignores, offends, or disrespects me, it is becoming easy for me to:

• Acknowledge my deepest core hurt and reconnect to my Core Value, regardless of what he/she says or does.	**Very true**	**True**	**Not Sure**	**Can't do it**
• Sympathize with the core hurt that motivated him/her.	**Very true**	**True**	**Not Sure**	**Can't do it**
• Attempt to solve problem in everyone's best interest.	**Very true**	**True**	**Not Sure**	**Can't do it**

DUE SESSION 5 **Name**

Perspective-Taking in Disputes

Describe, in as much detail as possible, the **perspective** or **point of view** of your **significant other, parent,** or **child** in a recent argument. (In describing it, do *not* **edit** it or **comment** on it, simply relate it ***the way he/she would.***)

What was his/her solution to this problem?

Which symptom or defense did he/she experience (anger, anxiety, obsessions, depression, manipulation, controlling behavior, etc.)?

Which was the deepest **core hurt** driving that person's behavior?

Did he or she feel that you understood him or her?

How would she (he) describe you at that moment, i.e., what did your behavior seem like to her or him?

Did you feel understood by her (him)?

What was your perspective of the same dispute?

What solution to this problem would you suggest now? (Keep in mind that anything worsening core hurts will fail).

DUE SESSION 5 **NAME**

HEALS™ LOG

I have rehearsed **HEALS™** ______ times this week (minimum 72 times). **HEALS™ requires *practice* to make it automatic and to get its full healing benefit.**

Write out the steps of **HEALS™**:

H-
E-
A-
L-
S-

I hurt the feelings of my significant other or children this week _____ (YES/No).
If no, congratulate yourself! If yes, how many times? _______

I hurt the body of my significant other or children this week _____ (YES/No).
If no, congratulate yourself! If yes, describe what you did:

Power Log

This week I felt:

• Irritable	**A lot**	**Some**	**Hardly**	**None**
• Grouchy	**A lot**	**Some**	**Hardly**	**None**
• Annoyed	**A lot**	**Some**	**Hardly**	**None**
• Impatient	**A lot**	**Some**	**Hardly**	**None**
• Angry in traffic	**A lot**	**Some**	**Hardly**	**None**
• Like blaming someone	**A lot**	**Some**	**Hardly**	**None**
• Like making other people do things	**A lot**	**Some**	**Hardly**	**None**
• Like getting revenge	**A lot**	**Some**	**Hardly**	**None**
• Like hurting someone	**A lot**	**Some**	**Hardly**	**None**

What always **motivates** my anger, attitude, anxiety, irritability, grouchiness, impatience, restlessness, impulse to blame, hurt, or desire to get revenge?

Someone else's behavior **my core hurt** **the situation**

What can I do to make it *better*?

Get back at them

Do HEALS™

Hope it will pass

What always motivates other people's attitudes, anger, anxiety, irritability, grouchiness, impatience, and restlessness or impulse to blame, hurt, or get revenge?

Someone else's behavior **their core hurts** **the situation**

What can I do to make it better?

Get back at them

Do HEALS™

Hope it will pass

Self-Concept (write out)

"I believe in my Core Value. I want to act in my long term and short term best interests."

Self-Esteem (write out)

"I accept myself, even if my behavior needs to change."

This week I felt the power to:

• Regulate anger, anxiety, attitudes, resentment	**A lot**	**Some**	**Hardly**	**None**
• Choose behaviors in short *and* long term best interest	**A lot**	**Some**	**Hardly**	**None**
• Be flexible (true to myself while adapting to others)	**A lot**	**Some**	**Hardly**	**None**
• Feel self-compassion (go deeper to reconnect to Core Value)	**A lot**	**Some**	**Hardly**	**None**
• Feel compassion for others (go deeper to validate their Core Value)	**A lot**	**Some**	**Hardly**	**None**

When someone ignores, offends, or disrespects me, it is becoming easy for me to:

• Acknowledge my deepest core hurt and reconnect to my Core Value, regardless of what he/she says or does.	**Very true**	**True**	**Not Sure**	**Can't do it**
• Sympathize with the core hurt that motivated him/her.	**Very true**	**True**	**Not Sure**	**Can't do it**
• Attempt to solve problem in everyone's best interest.	**Very true**	**True**	**Not Sure**	**Can't do it**

DUE SESSION 6 **Name**

Drilling Your New Skills

Briefly describe the worst dispute you ever had with your significant other, parent or child, when you got the angriest or most resentful.

Describe how this incident could have been improved using your new skill in emotional regulation?

DUE SESSION 6 **Name**

Based on past experience, I expect that my significant other will do the following things in the next week that will irritate me (or that used to irritate me). This is how I will react.

What she might do:

What I will do:

What she might do:

What I will do:

What she might do:

What I will do:

Based on past experience, I expect that that my children will do the following things in the next week that will irritate me (or that used to irritate me.) This is how I will react.

What they might do:

What I will do:

What they might do:

What I will do:

What they might do:

What I will do:

DUE SESSION 6 Name

HEALS™ LOG

I have rehearsed **HEALS™** ______ times this week (minimum 72 times). **HEALS™ requires *practice* to make it automatic and to get its full healing benefit.**

Write out the steps of **HEALS™**:

H-
E-
A-
L-
S-

I hurt the feelings of my significant other or children this week _____ (YES/No).
If no, congratulate yourself! If yes, how many times? _______

I hurt the body of my significant other or children this week _____ (YES/No).
If no, congratulate yourself! If yes, describe what you did:

Power Log

This week I felt:

• Irritable	**A lot**	**Some**	**Hardly**	**None**
• Grouchy	**A lot**	**Some**	**Hardly**	**None**
• Annoyed	**A lot**	**Some**	**Hardly**	**None**
• Impatient	**A lot**	**Some**	**Hardly**	**None**
• Angry in traffic	**A lot**	**Some**	**Hardly**	**None**
• Like blaming someone	**A lot**	**Some**	**Hardly**	**None**
• Like making other people do things	**A lot**	**Some**	**Hardly**	**None**
• Like getting revenge	**A lot**	**Some**	**Hardly**	**None**
• Like hurting someone	**A lot**	**Some**	**Hardly**	**None**

What always **motivates** my anger, attitude, anxiety, irritability, grouchiness, impatience, restlessness, impulse to blame, hurt, or desire to get revenge?

Someone else's behavior **my core hurt** **the situation**

What can I do to make it *better*?

Get back at them

Do HEALS™

Hope it will pass

What always motivates other people's attitudes, anger, anxiety, irritability, grouchiness, impatience, and restlessness or impulse to blame, hurt, or get revenge?

Someone else's behavior **their core hurts** **the situation**

What can I do to make it better?

Get back at them

Do HEALS™

Hope it will pass

Self-Concept (write out)

"I believe in my Core Value. I want to act in my long term and short term best interests."

Self-Esteem (write out)

"I accept myself, even if my behavior needs to change."

This week I felt the power to:

• Regulate anger, anxiety, attitudes, resentment	**A lot**	**Some**	**Hardly**	**None**
• Choose behaviors in short *and* long term best interest	**A lot**	**Some**	**Hardly**	**None**
• Be flexible (true to myself while adapting to others)	**A lot**	**Some**	**Hardly**	**None**
• Feel self-compassion (go deeper to reconnect to Core Value)	**A lot**	**Some**	**Hardly**	**None**
• Feel compassion for others (go deeper to validate their Core Value)	**A lot**	**Some**	**Hardly**	**None**

When someone ignores, offends, or disrespects me, it is becoming easy for me to:

• Acknowledge my deepest core hurt and reconnect to my Core Value, regardless of what he/she says or does.	**Very true**	**True**	**Not Sure**	**Can't do it**
• Sympathize with the core hurt that motivated him/her.	**Very true**	**True**	**Not Sure**	**Can't do it**
• Attempt to solve problem in everyone's best interest.	**Very true**	**True**	**Not Sure**	**Can't do it**

DUE SESSION 7 Name

HEALS™ LOG

I have rehearsed **HEALS™** ______ times this week (minimum 72 times). **HEALS™ requires *practice* to make it automatic and to get its full healing benefit.**

Write out the steps of **HEALS™**:

H-
E-
A-
L-
S-

I hurt the feelings of my significant other or children this week _____ (YES/No).
If no, congratulate yourself! If yes, how many times? _______

I hurt the body of my significant other or children this week _____ (YES/No).
If no, congratulate yourself! If yes, describe what you did:

Power Log

This week I felt:

• Irritable	**A lot**	**Some**	**Hardly**	**None**
• Grouchy	**A lot**	**Some**	**Hardly**	**None**
• Annoyed	**A lot**	**Some**	**Hardly**	**None**
• Impatient	**A lot**	**Some**	**Hardly**	**None**
• Angry in traffic	**A lot**	**Some**	**Hardly**	**None**
• Like blaming someone	**A lot**	**Some**	**Hardly**	**None**
• Like making other people do things	**A lot**	**Some**	**Hardly**	**None**
• Like getting revenge	**A lot**	**Some**	**Hardly**	**None**
• Like hurting someone	**A lot**	**Some**	**Hardly**	**None**

What always **motivates** my anger, attitude, anxiety, irritability, grouchiness, impatience, restlessness, impulse to blame, hurt, or desire to get revenge?

Someone else's behavior **my core hurt** **the situation**

What can I do to make it *better*?

Get back at them
Do HEALS™
Hope it will pass

What always motivates other people's attitudes, anger, anxiety, irritability, grouchiness, impatience, and restlessness or impulse to blame, hurt, or get revenge?

Someone else's behavior **their core hurts** **the situation**

What can I do to make it better?

Get back at them
Do HEALS™
Hope it will pass

Self-Concept (write out)

"I believe in my Core Value. I want to act in my long term and short term best interests."

Self-Esteem (write out)

"I accept myself, even if my behavior needs to change."

This week I felt the power to:

• Regulate anger, anxiety, attitudes, resentment	**A lot**	**Some**	**Hardly**	**None**
• Choose behaviors in short *and* long term best interest	**A lot**	**Some**	**Hardly**	**None**
• Be flexible (true to myself while adapting to others)	**A lot**	**Some**	**Hardly**	**None**
• Feel self-compassion (go deeper to reconnect to Core Value)	**A lot**	**Some**	**Hardly**	**None**
• Feel compassion for others (go deeper to validate their Core Value)	**A lot**	**Some**	**Hardly**	**None**

When someone ignores, offends, or disrespects me, it is becoming easy for me to:

• Acknowledge my deepest core hurt and reconnect to my Core Value, regardless of what he/she says or does.	**Very true**	**True**	**Not Sure**	**Can't do it**
• Sympathize with the core hurt that motivated him/her.	**Very true**	**True**	**Not Sure**	**Can't do it**
• Attempt to solve problem in everyone's best interest.	**Very true**	**True**	**Not Sure**	**Can't do it**

DUE SESSION 8 Name

HEALS™ LOG

I have rehearsed **HEALS™** ______ times this week (minimum 72 times). **HEALS™ requires *practice* to make it automatic and to get its full healing benefit.**

Write out the steps of **HEALS™**:

H-
E-
A-
L-
S-

I hurt the feelings of my significant other or children this week _____ (YES/No).
If no, congratulate yourself! If yes, how many times? _______

I hurt the body of my significant other or children this week _____ (YES/No).
If no, congratulate yourself! If yes, describe what you did:

Power Log

This week I felt:

• Irritable	**A lot**	**Some**	**Hardly**	**None**
• Grouchy	**A lot**	**Some**	**Hardly**	**None**
• Annoyed	**A lot**	**Some**	**Hardly**	**None**
• Impatient	**A lot**	**Some**	**Hardly**	**None**
• Angry in traffic	**A lot**	**Some**	**Hardly**	**None**
• Like blaming someone	**A lot**	**Some**	**Hardly**	**None**
• Like making other people do things	**A lot**	**Some**	**Hardly**	**None**
• Like getting revenge	**A lot**	**Some**	**Hardly**	**None**
• Like hurting someone	**A lot**	**Some**	**Hardly**	**None**

What always **motivates** my anger, attitude, anxiety, irritability, grouchiness, impatience, restlessness, impulse to blame, hurt, or desire to get revenge?

Someone else's behavior **my core hurt** **the situation**

What can I do to make it *better*?

Get back at them

Do HEALS™

Hope it will pass

What always motivates other people's attitudes, anger, anxiety, irritability, grouchiness, impatience, and restlessness or impulse to blame, hurt, or get revenge?

Someone else's behavior **their core hurts** **the situation**

What can I do to make it better?

Get back at them

Do HEALS™

Hope it will pass

Self-Concept (write out)

"I believe in my Core Value. I want to act in my long term and short term best interests."

Self-Esteem (write out)

"I accept myself, even if my behavior needs to change."

This week I felt the power to:

• Regulate anger, anxiety, attitudes, resentment	**A lot**	**Some**	**Hardly**	**None**
• Choose behaviors in short *and* long term best interest	**A lot**	**Some**	**Hardly**	**None**
• Be flexible (true to myself while adapting to others)	**A lot**	**Some**	**Hardly**	**None**
• Feel self-compassion (go deeper to reconnect to Core Value)	**A lot**	**Some**	**Hardly**	**None**
• Feel compassion for others (go deeper to validate their Core Value)	**A lot**	**Some**	**Hardly**	**None**

When someone ignores, offends, or disrespects me, it is becoming easy for me to:

• Acknowledge my deepest core hurt and reconnect to my Core Value, regardless of what he/she says or does.	**Very true**	**True**	**Not Sure**	**Can't do it**
• Sympathize with the core hurt that motivated him/her.	**Very true**	**True**	**Not Sure**	**Can't do it**
• Attempt to solve problem in everyone's best interest.	**Very true**	**True**	**Not Sure**	**Can't do it**

DUE SESSION 9 **Name**

Evaluating Your Attachment Bond

The following are questions you must answer from deep in your heart.

1. How much do you love this person?

2. Is the attachment bond between you a strong one?

3. Or is it maintained by habit, convenience, or coercion?

4. Is the damage done to the relationship repairable?

5. Do you *want* to repair it?

6. How can it be repaired?

7. How will you know that it is being repaired? (There must be positive improvement, not just, "We don't fight as much," or, "He/she isn't so mean to me anymore.")

8. What will you do differently when it is repaired?

9. How can you go forward, growing from the hurt of the past? (You must grow to heal, whether your loved ones grow with you or not.)

DUE SESSION 9 **Name**

Supporting the Attachment Bond

Whether we like it or not, a bond forms between people in attachment relationships. We can attack and resent the bond or enhance and support it. Even if you don't have a spouse/significant other or children, **answer as if you did.**

List at least five things you can do to enhance and support your attachment bond with your significant other.

1.

2.

3.

4.

5.

List at least five things you can do to enhance and support your attachment bond with your children or parents.

1.

2.

3.

4.

5.

DUE SESSION 9 **Name**

HEALS™ LOG

I have rehearsed **HEALS™** ______ times this week (minimum 72 times). **HEALS™ requires *practice* to make it automatic and to get its full healing benefit.**

Write out the steps of **HEALS™**:

H-
E-
A-
L-
S-

I hurt the feelings of my significant other or children this week _____ (YES/No).
If no, congratulate yourself! If yes, how many times? _______

I hurt the body of my significant other or children this week _____ (YES/No).
If no, congratulate yourself! If yes, describe what you did:

Power Log

This week I felt:

• Irritable	**A lot**	**Some**	**Hardly**	**None**
• Grouchy	**A lot**	**Some**	**Hardly**	**None**
• Annoyed	**A lot**	**Some**	**Hardly**	**None**
• Impatient	**A lot**	**Some**	**Hardly**	**None**
• Angry in traffic	**A lot**	**Some**	**Hardly**	**None**
• Like blaming someone	**A lot**	**Some**	**Hardly**	**None**
• Like making other people do things	**A lot**	**Some**	**Hardly**	**None**
• Like getting revenge	**A lot**	**Some**	**Hardly**	**None**
• Like hurting someone	**A lot**	**Some**	**Hardly**	**None**

What always **motivates** my anger, attitude, anxiety, irritability, grouchiness, impatience, restlessness, impulse to blame, hurt, or desire to get revenge?

Someone else's behavior **my core hurt** **the situation**

What can I do to make it *better*?

Get back at them
Do HEALS™
Hope it will pass

What always motivates other people's attitudes, anger, anxiety, irritability, grouchiness, impatience, and restlessness or impulse to blame, hurt, or get revenge?

Someone else's behavior **their core hurts** **the situation**

What can I do to make it better?

Get back at them
Do HEALS™
Hope it will pass

Self-Concept (write out)

"I believe in my Core Value. I want to act in my long term and short term best interests."

Self-Esteem (write out)

"I accept myself, even if my behavior needs to change."

This week I felt the power to:

• Regulate anger, anxiety, attitudes, resentment	**A lot**	**Some**	**Hardly**	**None**
• Choose behaviors in short *and* long term best interest	**A lot**	**Some**	**Hardly**	**None**
• Be flexible (true to myself while adapting to others)	**A lot**	**Some**	**Hardly**	**None**
• Feel self-compassion (go deeper to reconnect to Core Value)	**A lot**	**Some**	**Hardly**	**None**
• Feel compassion for others (go deeper to validate their Core Value)	**A lot**	**Some**	**Hardly**	**None**

When someone ignores, offends, or disrespects me, it is becoming easy for me to:

• Acknowledge my deepest core hurt and reconnect to my Core Value, regardless of what he/she says or does.	**Very true**	**True**	**Not Sure**	**Can't do it**
• Sympathize with the core hurt that motivated him/her.	**Very true**	**True**	**Not Sure**	**Can't do it**
• Attempt to solve problem in everyone's best interest.	**Very true**	**True**	**Not Sure**	**Can't do it**

DUE SESSION 10 **Name**

HEALS™ LOG

I have rehearsed **HEALS™** ______ times this week (minimum 72 times). **HEALS™ requires *practice* to make it automatic and to get its full healing benefit.**

Write out the steps of **HEALS™**:

H-
E-
A-
L-
S-

I hurt the feelings of my significant other or children this week _____ (YES/No).
If no, congratulate yourself! If yes, how many times? _______

I hurt the body of my significant other or children this week _____ (YES/No).
If no, congratulate yourself! If yes, describe what you did:

Power Log

This week I felt:

• Irritable	**A lot**	**Some**	**Hardly**	**None**
• Grouchy	**A lot**	**Some**	**Hardly**	**None**
• Annoyed	**A lot**	**Some**	**Hardly**	**None**
• Impatient	**A lot**	**Some**	**Hardly**	**None**
• Angry in traffic	**A lot**	**Some**	**Hardly**	**None**
• Like blaming someone	**A lot**	**Some**	**Hardly**	**None**
• Like making other people do things	**A lot**	**Some**	**Hardly**	**None**
• Like getting revenge	**A lot**	**Some**	**Hardly**	**None**
• Like hurting someone	**A lot**	**Some**	**Hardly**	**None**

What always **motivates** my anger, attitude, anxiety, irritability, grouchiness, impatience, restlessness, impulse to blame, hurt, or desire to get revenge?

Someone else's behavior **my core hurt** **the situation**

What can I do to make it *better*?

Get back at them
Do HEALS™
Hope it will pass

What always motivates other people's attitudes, anger, anxiety, irritability, grouchiness, impatience, and restlessness or impulse to blame, hurt, or get revenge?

Someone else's behavior **their core hurts** **the situation**

What can I do to make it better?

Get back at them
Do HEALS™
Hope it will pass

Self-Concept (write out)

"I believe in my Core Value. I want to act in my long term and short term best interests."

Self-Esteem (write out)

"I accept myself, even if my behavior needs to change."

This week I felt the power to:

• Regulate anger, anxiety, attitudes, resentment	**A lot**	**Some**	**Hardly**	**None**
• Choose behaviors in short *and* long term best interest	**A lot**	**Some**	**Hardly**	**None**
• Be flexible (true to myself while adapting to others)	**A lot**	**Some**	**Hardly**	**None**
• Feel self-compassion (go deeper to reconnect to Core Value)	**A lot**	**Some**	**Hardly**	**None**
• Feel compassion for others (go deeper to validate their Core Value)	**A lot**	**Some**	**Hardly**	**None**

When someone ignores, offends, or disrespects me, it is becoming easy for me to:

• Acknowledge my deepest core hurt and reconnect to my Core Value, regardless of what he/she says or does.	**Very true**	**True**	**Not Sure**	**Can't do it**
• Sympathize with the core hurt that motivated him/her.	**Very true**	**True**	**Not Sure**	**Can't do it**
• Attempt to solve problem in everyone's best interest.	**Very true**	**True**	**Not Sure**	**Can't do it**

DUE SESSION 11 **Name**

Resentment List

List the things you resent about work, coworkers, bosses, family, and friends. For maximum benefit of this exercise, be as thorough and honest as you can.

When you have finished, read your list **slowly** and **out loud**. Use another sheet of paper if necessary.

1. I resent
2. I resent
3. I resent
4. I resent
5. I resent
6. I resent
7. I resent
8. I resent
9. I resent
10. I resent

DUE SESSION 11 **Name**

Power

Write what you can do to improve (not necessarily "fix") the items on your resentment list. **Note:** "Ignoring it" improves nothing.

This is what *I* can do to improve **my experience** of item #1 on my resentment list.

This is what *I* can do to improve **my experience** of item #2 on my resentment list.

This is what *I* can do to improve **my experience** of item #3 on my resentment list.

This is what *I* can do to improve **my experience** of item #4 on my resentment list.

This is what *I* can do to improve **my experience** of item #5 on my resentment list.

This is what *I* can do to improve **my experience** of item #6 on my resentment list.

This is what *I* can do to improve **my experience** of item #7 on my resentment list.

This is what *I* can do to improve **my experience** of item #8 on my resentment list.

This is what *I* can do to improve **my experience** of item #9 on my resentment list.

This is what I can do to improve **my experience** of item #10 on my resentment list.

DUE SESSION 11 **Name**

Power II

Identify the *deepest* core hurt stimulated by each item on your resentment list. By forgiving yourself for allowing your Core Value to be lowered, you take back power over your emotional well being.

Item 1. I forgive myself for losing sight of my Core Value and feeling (name core hurt): __________________________, when he/she _______________________________.

Item 2. I forgive myself for losing sight of my Core Value and feeling (name core hurt): __________________________, when he/she _______________________________.

Item 3. I forgive myself for losing sight of my Core Value and feeling (name core hurt): __________________________, when he/she _______________________________.

Item 4. I forgive myself for losing sight of my Core Value and feeling (name core hurt): __________________________, when he/she _______________________________.

Item 5. I forgive myself for losing sight of my Core Value and feeling (name core hurt): __________________________, when he/she _______________________________.

Item 6. I forgive myself for losing sight of my Core Value and feeling (name core hurt): __________________________, when he/she _______________________________.

Item 7. I forgive myself for losing sight of my Core Value and feeling (name core hurt): __________________________, when he/she _______________________________.

Item 8. I forgive myself for losing sight of my Core Value and feeling (name core hurt): __________________________, when he/she _______________________________.

Item 9. I forgive myself for losing sight of my Core Value and feeling (name core hurt): __________________________, when he/she _______________________________.

Item 10. I forgive myself for losing sight of my Core Value and feeling (name core hurt): __________________________, when he/she _______________________________.

DUE SESSION 11 **Name**

The Road to Power: Forgiveness of Others

Forgiveness does not mean condoning bad behavior, overlooking an offense, or reinstating a relationship.

Forgiveness means forgoing the impulse to punish, in recognition of the harm it does to the self.

Item 1. I forgive you for reminding me that I sometimes feel (name core hurt): ________________.

Item 2. I forgive you for reminding me that I sometimes feel (name core hurt): ________________.

Item 3. I forgive you for reminding me that I sometimes feel (name core hurt): ________________.

Item 4. I forgive you for reminding me that I sometimes feel (name core hurt): ________________.

Item 5. I forgive you for reminding me that I sometimes feel (name core hurt): ________________.

Item 6. I forgive you for reminding me that I sometimes feel (name core hurt): ________________.

Item 7. I forgive you for reminding me that I sometimes feel (name core hurt): ________________.

Item 8. I forgive you for reminding me that I sometimes feel (name core hurt): ________________.

Item 9. I forgive you for reminding me that I sometimes feel (name core hurt): ________________.

Item 10. I forgive you for reminding me that I sometimes feel (name core hurt): ________________.

DUE SESSION 11 Name

HEALS™ LOG

I have rehearsed **HEALS™** ______ times this week (minimum 72 times). **HEALS™ requires *practice* to make it automatic and to get its full healing benefit.**

Write out the steps of **HEALS™**:

H-
E-
A-
L-
S-

I hurt the feelings of my significant other or children this week _____ (YES/No).
If no, congratulate yourself! If yes, how many times? ______

I hurt the body of my significant other or children this week _____ (YES/No).
If no, congratulate yourself! If yes, describe what you did:

Power Log

This week I felt:

• Irritable	**A lot**	**Some**	**Hardly**	**None**
• Grouchy	**A lot**	**Some**	**Hardly**	**None**
• Annoyed	**A lot**	**Some**	**Hardly**	**None**
• Impatient	**A lot**	**Some**	**Hardly**	**None**
• Angry in traffic	**A lot**	**Some**	**Hardly**	**None**
• Like blaming someone	**A lot**	**Some**	**Hardly**	**None**
• Like making other people do things	**A lot**	**Some**	**Hardly**	**None**
• Like getting revenge	**A lot**	**Some**	**Hardly**	**None**
• Like hurting someone	**A lot**	**Some**	**Hardly**	**None**

What always **motivates** my anger, attitude, anxiety, irritability, grouchiness, impatience, restlessness, impulse to blame, hurt, or desire to get revenge?

Someone else's behavior **my core hurt** **the situation**

What can I do to make it *better*?

Get back at them
Do HEALS™
Hope it will pass

What always motivates other people's attitudes, anger, anxiety, irritability, grouchiness, impatience, and restlessness or impulse to blame, hurt, or get revenge?

Someone else's behavior | **their core hurts** | **the situation**

What can I do to make it better?

Get back at them
Do HEALS™
Hope it will pass

Self-Concept (write out)

"I believe in my Core Value. I want to act in my long term and short term best interests."

Self-Esteem (write out)

"I accept myself, even if my behavior needs to change."

This week I felt the power to:

• Regulate anger, anxiety, attitudes, resentment	**A lot**	**Some**	**Hardly**	**None**
• Choose behaviors in short *and* long term best interest	**A lot**	**Some**	**Hardly**	**None**
• Be flexible (true to myself while adapting to others)	**A lot**	**Some**	**Hardly**	**None**
• Feel self-compassion (go deeper to reconnect to Core Value)	**A lot**	**Some**	**Hardly**	**None**
• Feel compassion for others (go deeper to validate their Core Value)	**A lot**	**Some**	**Hardly**	**None**

When someone ignores, offends, or disrespects me, it is becoming easy for me to:

• Acknowledge my deepest core hurt and reconnect to my Core Value, regardless of what he/she says or does.	**Very true**	**True**	**Not Sure**	**Can't do it**
• Sympathize with the core hurt that motivated him/her.	**Very true**	**True**	**Not Sure**	**Can't do it**
• Attempt to solve problem in everyone's best interest.	**Very true**	**True**	**Not Sure**	**Can't do it**

DUE SESSION 12 **Name**

Consolidating Gains

You have learned a deeper understanding of your thoughts, feelings, behavior, goals, and motivations. You have learned a deeper level of communicating. Now it's crucial to consolidate your gains.

Write what you have gained from this therapeutic experience. Then recite your list aloud – it's important that you hear your voice consolidating your gains.

Include the following items in your list:

- The relationship of compassion and anger
- How compassion works as a defense
- The most efficient means of avoiding power struggles
- The difference between blame and responsibility
- Genuine pride and self-esteem vs. false pride and self-esteem
- How to resolve resentment
- What does alcohol and drug use do to emotional regulation skill?
- What else have you learned?

DUE SESSION 12 **Name**

Core Value Workshop Final Examination

1. How will you handle your spouse/significant other disagreeing with something important to you?

   If you can't reach an agreement, to what extent can you tolerate disagreement?

   What will you do if you *cannot* tolerate disagreement?

2. Your spouse/significant other says or does something disrespectful to you. What internal experience does that stimulate in you?

   What internal experience in him/her motivated his/her behavior?

   How will you respond?

   Your child does or says something disrespectful to you. What internal experience does that stimulate in you?

   What internal experience in him/her motivated his/her behavior?

   How will you respond?

3. When your core hurts flare up, whether on their own or in response to something your spouse/significant other or child does, what will you do?

How can you reconnect to your Core Value?

How can you validate the Core Value of loved ones?

4. You see your spouse/significant other flirt with someone at a party. What will you do?

What will you do if your spouse/significant other seems uncomfortable telling you where she/he has been?

5. What is the difference between a behavior-request and telling your spouse/significant other to do something?

Is there any justification for telling him/her what to do?

Will telling him/her what to do be effective in the long run?

6. Is there justification for saying negative things about your ex-spouse/significant other in front of your children?

Is there justification for using children to get at an ex-spouse/significant other?

7. Is it possible for anyone to make you feel an emotion that you cannot regulate?

8. What circumstances justify hitting a spouse/significant other or child?

   What circumstances justify verbal aggression (threats, name-calling, humiliation, insults, harsh criticism, any kind of criticism about the person rather than behavior) against a spouse/significant other or child?

9. What circumstances justify attempts to control the behavior of a spouse/significant other?

10. What are the three elements of self-building in attachment relationships?

1.

2.

3.

11. How will you guarantee safety, security, and compassion in your present or next relationship with a spouse/significant other?

    With your children?

12. What is post traumatic stress?

    Why does it make recovery from abuse so slow and difficult?

DUE SESSION 12 **Name**

HEALS™ LOG

I have rehearsed **HEALS™** ______ times this week (minimum 72 times). **HEALS™ requires *practice* to make it automatic and to get its full healing benefit.**

Write out the steps of **HEALS™**:

H-
E-
A-
L-
S-

I hurt the feelings of my significant other or children this week _____ (YES/No).
If no, congratulate yourself! If yes, how many times? ______

I hurt the body of my significant other or children this week _____ (YES/No).
If no, congratulate yourself! If yes, describe what you did:

Power Log

This week I felt:

• Irritable	**A lot**	**Some**	**Hardly**	**None**
• Grouchy	**A lot**	**Some**	**Hardly**	**None**
• Annoyed	**A lot**	**Some**	**Hardly**	**None**
• Impatient	**A lot**	**Some**	**Hardly**	**None**
• Angry in traffic	**A lot**	**Some**	**Hardly**	**None**
• Like blaming someone	**A lot**	**Some**	**Hardly**	**None**
• Like making other people do things	**A lot**	**Some**	**Hardly**	**None**
• Like getting revenge	**A lot**	**Some**	**Hardly**	**None**
• Like hurting someone	**A lot**	**Some**	**Hardly**	**None**

What always **motivates** my anger, attitude, anxiety, irritability, grouchiness, impatience, restlessness, impulse to blame, hurt, or desire to get revenge?

Someone else's behavior **my core hurt** **the situation**

What can I do to make it *better*?

Get back at them
Do HEALS™
Hope it will pass

What always motivates other people's attitudes, anger, anxiety, irritability, grouchiness, impatience, and restlessness or impulse to blame, hurt, or get revenge?

Someone else's behavior **their core hurts** **the situation**

What can I do to make it better?

Get back at them
Do HEALS™
Hope it will pass

Self-Concept (write out)

"I believe in my Core Value. I want to act in my long term and short term best interests."

Self-Esteem (write out)

"I accept myself, even if my behavior needs to change."

This week I felt the power to:

• Regulate anger, anxiety, attitudes, resentment	**A lot**	**Some**	**Hardly**	**None**
• Choose behaviors in short *and* long term best interest	**A lot**	**Some**	**Hardly**	**None**
• Be flexible (true to myself while adapting to others)	**A lot**	**Some**	**Hardly**	**None**
• Feel self-compassion (go deeper to reconnect to Core Value)	**A lot**	**Some**	**Hardly**	**None**
• Feel compassion for others (go deeper to validate their Core Value)	**A lot**	**Some**	**Hardly**	**None**

When someone ignores, offends, or disrespects me, it is becoming easy for me to:

• Acknowledge my deepest core hurt and reconnect to my Core Value, regardless of what he/she says or does.	**Very true**	**True**	**Not Sure**	**Can't do it**
• Sympathize with the core hurt that motivated him/her.	**Very true**	**True**	**Not Sure**	**Can't do it**
• Attempt to solve problem in everyone's best interest.	**Very true**	**True**	**Not Sure**	**Can't do it**

Made in the USA